ALLAYNE L. WEBSTER

OUR LITTLE SECRET

fi

This book is intended for a Young Adult audience.
Trigger Warning: Sexual abuse and rape are depicted.

This is a work of fiction.
All names, characters and places are fictitious.

Teaching Notes are available at www.ligatu.re
and www.allaynewebster.com.

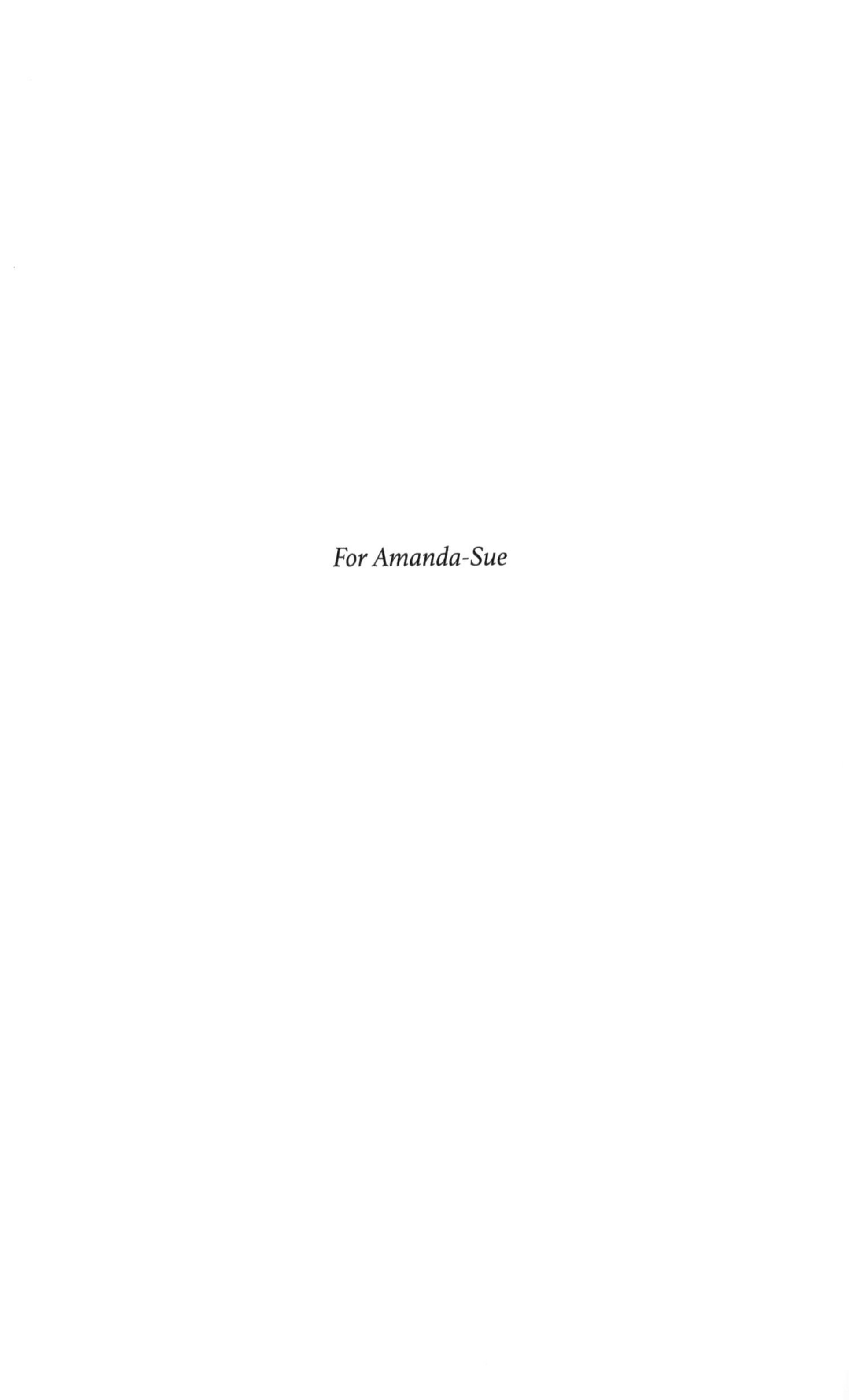

For Amanda-Sue

FOREWORD BY ALLAYNE WEBSTER

Our Little Secret was contracted by Dyan Blacklock, Publisher at Omnibus Scholastic, and was first released almost fifteen years ago. *Speak* by Laurie Halse Anderson had been published to wide acclaim in 1999; I knew I had written a similarly affecting story, but I didn't think I was breaking any new ground. When I signed the contract, I was told my novel might not be marketed in the traditional sense because of its challenging content, but it was important to publish it nonetheless.

Not long after *Our Little Secret* was released, I became aware of an underground banned and challenged book list (supposedly such lists do not exist in Australia). My novel was on it, and I was devastated. There was no #MeToo movement then, but the tide was turning—there was more frequent representation and more open discussion surrounding rape, sexual abuse and consent in YA fiction. But, as I progressed in my career as an author, visiting schools and speaking to students about my books, I was regularly asked not to talk about *Our Little Secret*.

In the years since *Our Little Secret* was published, I've lost count of the number of requests for copies I've received from readers who had read it in high school, despite the novel being held 'under the counter'. Both young people and adults took this book into their hearts—they remember fourteen-year-old Edwina Saltmarsh's story. Some early reviews declared Edwina 'naïve'; inherent in that judgement is that Edwina's naïveté makes her to somehow to blame—or complicit—in the sexual abuse and rape she suffers. It's true: Edwina *is* naive. She is a child, an innocent in both a literal and a lawful sense, a child who lacks the experience to understand what is happening to her. Her trust has been betrayed, and the only way to survive is to keep her abuser's secret.

Edwina's story can be a confronting read, but it's important we speak more openly about consent. The lines are not blurred, as some would suggest, and there should be clear boundaries—but these conversations can only take place if voices like Edwina's are not silenced. In asking me not to talk about this book, Edwina's voice was silenced a second time. This new edition of *Our Little Secret* means we can talk about it now—today—because its relevance has not diminished over time.

Our Little Secret is a story about exposing the truth. It's about courage, healing, and the enduring power of the human spirit. Most of all, this novel celebrates friendship and hope. While minor revisions have been made to reflect a more contemporary understanding of victim blaming, slut-shaming, gaslighting, and other methods used to control women and their sexuality, the original text remains largely unchanged.

This is not a story every girl should read, as the original blurb suggested, but a story everyone should read. Let's talk.

Predators come in all shapes and sizes. They don't always lurk in shadows. They walk among us. Sometimes they take the form of a loved one or a family friend. We are taught to trust. Taught to have faith in people. Taught to love. So we open the door wide to let others in. We don't realise we've let in a predator until it's too late.

PROLOGUE

When the news swept the little town of Wattleton that sixteen-year-old Anne-Marie Cooper had been raped on her way home from school one summer afternoon, some townsfolk said they weren't surprised. They could have seen it coming. Some even said that Anne-Marie had asked for it. I know this, because one of those people was my own mother.

To say any woman had asked to be raped—well, that's just stupid. But my mother didn't let the facts get in the way of a good story. Not since the local preacher's wife was booked for drink-driving had she had such a juicy story on which to speculate.

Anne-Marie is the elder sister of my best friend Becky, and from what I knew, she hadn't even kissed a boy. Becky says Anne-Marie has a huge crush on Mr Whitelock, who teaches gym class at Wattleton High. Mr Whitelock is kind of handsome I guess, but not *that* handsome.

What I know about what happened to Anne-Marie isn't much, to be honest. Most of what I heard came from Sarah Langhorn, who'd heard the story from her mother. Sarah's mother had heard it from Mrs Crocker, who was the sister of Mrs Dobson, who was married to the local copper. And if that doesn't boggle your brain, Sarah Langhorn reckons Mrs Dobson didn't hear it from her husband, but instead secretly checked out the case file he brought home from work one evening. She'd told her sister not to say anything, but you know country towns—there isn't any such thing as a secret, just deluded people thinking they can keep one. You might ask why I hadn't heard about it from Becky. Well, that's because Becky hadn't been to school since it happened, and my mother wouldn't let me call her because she said Mrs Cooper might think we were being nosy. Can you believe it?

So what I do know, reliable or not, is that Anne-Marie had been walking home from school on a Friday afternoon, and as she crossed the old football oval headed for the main street of Wattleton, a bloke—who was believed to be from out of town—dragged her into the back of an old station wagon and well, you know ... I even heard Anne-Marie had been knocked out and had a scar on her head to prove it, but I can't be sure that bit was true because Sarah Langhorn has a habit of embellishing her stories. Anyway, I ask you: if some stranger had attacked Anne-Marie, how can that show Anne-Marie was asking for it?

My mum said that Mrs Cooper had always allowed Anne-Marie to wear her skirts too high and had let her daughter become far too familiar with the local footy players for a girl her age. This was, apparently, a red flag to the bull of unwanted male attention. She was asking for it. According to Mum, Mrs Cooper had been exactly the same in her day—flirting with the boys outside the corner store, accepting rides from local hooligans, lifting the hem of her school dress to reveal her knees. No wonder Anne-Marie had fallen out of the same biscuit cutter.

In a town like Wattleton, everyone knew everything there was to know about everyone else. All the same, Becky was probably embarrassed that the whole town was talking about her family.

What must it have been like for Anne-Marie? What a thing to go through. She would have been walking through the thick weedy grass of the old footy oval carrying her backpack full of textbooks, maybe daydreaming about Mr Whitelock and gym class. She was probably headed for the local bakery, already tasting the luscious cream of a Wattleton sugar bun. Or perhaps she was tallying up in her head her homework load for the night, thinking about the topic for her biology research project.

She must have walked a little too close to the pine trees that surrounded the oval, their enormous branches plunging her in shadows, the sun finding her again as she surfaced spasmodically between them.

He must have been waiting for her there.

CHAPTER 1

My whole family was late for church. Again. Like we arrived anywhere on time. We were always slinking up the aisles when the hymns had already started, picking our way over people's legs and handbags to find a seat. My mum would point across the tiny church to vacant pews. There was rarely one left for us to sit in as a family. My brothers would peer back over their shoulders, searching for the rest of us. Mum would scowl at them and mouth, *Turn around*. Madeline Abbott saw my mum and promptly turned up her nose. Madeline saw everything, heard everything, and knew *everything* about everyone else. She might as well have been God Himself.

Our church was small. The elders had begun to replace some of the pews with plastic chairs and mismatched cushions. One of the windows had been smashed by vandals, and the plastic garbage bag that was taped to the window frame sucked in and out with the wind. Needless to say, the noise made quiet prayer almost impossible. The floor was lined with matted old carpet that had definitely seen better days. A huge cross of brown wood veneer adorned the wall at the front with fluoro lights behind it giving off an obviously artificial yellow glow. Below that was a table with the cup of Christ that Reverend Lockhardt always got to drink from. The rest of us got tiny plastic cups filled with the blood of Christ—or something that looked and smelt kind of suspicious.

Eighty-six-year-old Margaret Taper played the church organ with vigour. She travelled for two hours every Sunday to get to church, driving her faithful 1961 EK Holden. My dad told me that Margaret skinned foxes and went roo shooting. I often wondered if the fur stole she wore to church was some poor animal she had hunted down.

I cursed my mum under my breath. Today she had made me wear long white socks with my favourite red mini skirt. She was so unforgivably daggy. I swear, she dressed me like I was ten years old instead of fourteen. No other fourteen-year-old I knew was dressed by her mother. I wanted to die every time I looked at my socks. I wondered if rolling them over would work. I decided to try, bending over to fold the first layer.

I don't know why I did it. The organ music started and I stood up, but kind of kept bent over at the same time, still rolling my sock. Madeline Abbott dug me in the ribs and I belted my head against the pew in front of me. It made a terrible thud, and the whole row turned around to look, still singing 'Onward Christian Soldiers'. I dared to peer back at Mum, whose face was livid. I knew then that the journey home would be a lecture on how we kids are *so* embarrassing, and *why* can't we just act like other people's kids for just one day? And was there *ever* a time when we went to church when we didn't do something that mortified her in public? And how *next time* she wouldn't bring any of us and just go by herself. If only. Jesus Christ, my head hurt.

I wondered if God knew I had just sworn in my head at church. Maybe He was too busy looking at little Robbie Cox, who was quietly sneaking coins from the collection tray. I tried that once. I nearly choked to death on the lolly I bought that afternoon with the money. Retribution, I guess.

'Edwina Saltmarsh!'

Oh God. It was Cecile Campbell calling my name over the microphone.

'Edwina, would you like to join the other children down the front here? It's time for God's Little Kingdom.' The microphone squealed with feedback, and Cecile leapt around frantically. Her thick reading glasses slipped down the ridge of her nose. As if I wanted to be part of God's Little Kingdom. I was thinking, are you people a bunch of freaks? Didn't one person in the whole room recognise that I had breasts? For the love of God,

I was fourteen! I'd been reading *Dolly* magazine for two years already. I saw my mum's face, and I could swear I saw a hint of smoke weaving its way from her ears. I moved down to the front of the room and sat cross-legged on the floor.

Mum was rostered to serve tea and coffee after church. Lining the tables were cakes and biscuits that I'd seen in her *Women's Weekly*. My brother George made the mistake of swiping a fairy cake before the church elders had said grace. Mr Harper biffed him across the top of his head, spilling his blond hair into his eyes. George held on to the cake for dear life and scampered off to the corner of the room to demolish it.

'Edwina dear, your mother wants to speak to you in the kitchen.' Mrs Appleton pointed towards the serving window.

'Edwina!' Mum hissed as I approached her. 'Where's Matthew?'

'I don't know.'

'Well, find him! Can't you even think to keep your eye on your brother for five minutes while I'm doing this? You are *so* self-involved.'

I looked at her, mustering my best *I know nothing* look.

'There you go, Mr Carter—would you like sugar with that?' She turned back to me. 'Look, Edwina—I'm tired. All I ask you to do is keep an eye on your brothers until I'm finished—maybe another twenty minutes. And for God's sake, pull your sock up. Hello there, Mrs Smith. How's Stewart doing after that awful accident? I heard it will take months for his leg to heal ... One black tea?'

'Mum, after church, can I go to Becky's house?'

'No, Edwina. I get sick to death of driving you around all day. It's Sunday. You can stay home for once—it won't kill you.'

'But—'

'Go and look after your brothers and leave me alone for five seconds, will you? I'll come and get you when I'm ready. Good morning, Reverend Lockhardt. It was a lovely service—I enjoyed it immensely. The part about patience and forgiveness really spoke to my soul.' She batted her eyelids at him.

'Well, that's good to hear, Mary. We aim to please! Hello there, Edwina.' Reverend Lockhardt winked at me.

'Hello, Reverend.'

'Edwina, please go and find Matthew, there's a good girl. She's such a wonderful help to me, Reverend Lockhardt—you have no idea.' Yeah, no idea she was Jekyll and Hyde.

I went outside and found Matthew scurrying in and out of the shrubs, playing with some kids. George was still inside attempting the world cupcake face-stuffing record. Nobody from my school went to my church, thank the Lord. I bet Kylie Baxter, who was, like, the coolest girl in school, didn't have to endure sermons longer than *War and Peace* every Sunday morning. I'd die if she saw me here. Church was not a place to be caught dead in. Well, except for the dead person in a funeral, I guess.

I sat on the stone steps of the Manse and kicked the gravel. This town is so boring. No one ever comes back once they move away. As soon as I was old enough, I was moving to the city. I was going to go to university to study art and travel the world. I was also going to become really, really rich. Only after I had painted in every city across Europe would I find a man and live in sin, and certainly not before the age of at least thirty. That was my grand plan, anyway. I wasn't going to be stuck here in Wattleton—that was for sure.

My mum grew up in Wattleton. She started dating my dad in high school. She said she had planned to go to the city and study nursing when she finished school, but my dad wanted to stay to work in the vineyards. Two months after finishing high school, my mum found out she was pregnant with me.

Mum said Wattleton was a good place to raise a family. She said most people went to church and had good Christian values.

My dad didn't care much for my mum's 'churchy stuff', as he called it. As long as she let him have his carton of beer every week he was happy. And as long as he didn't mention the beer and he came to church with her on Sundays, she was happy.

Anyway, when Mum started on about her churchy stuff, I would escape to my room to do my homework—or at least that was my excuse. No one I knew had *that* much homework. Most of the time I just read *Dolly* magazine.

I started buying *Dolly* with the pocket money Nanna gave me. *Dolly* said oversized sunglasses were the rage. I had some that Mum bought me from the chemist gift shop. I practically had to beg her, but I knew Mum would give in if I asked her really loudly in front of the chemist shop ladies, who were watching us. *Dolly* said you should wear oversized sunglasses teamed with a thick headscarf. Apparently that looked cool. Apparently straightening your hair with a straightening iron was also cool, hence I straightened my hair every morning. There was a lot about fashion to remember.

Dolly not only had fashion tips—it had stories about sex! My mum didn't want to talk about sex. I remember our one and only 'sex talk'. She sat me down one day at the kitchen table and explained reproduction. Firstly, she talked about the menstrual cycle and a bunch of stuff I already knew from health science class. I didn't interrupt her, though, because it was the first time she had ever wanted to tell me anything like this. She said she thought I was at the age where I could start being treated like an adult.

Mum said the first person she had sex with was my dad, and that was the only person she had ever slept with. (Gross! As if I wanted to know about my parents doing it!) She said that God only intended for you to do it with one person—your husband. She said she hoped I would wait until I met the man I wanted to marry. She said I could do things like kiss and hold hands until then. That would make her proud of me. She also said I shouldn't brag about the things I do with boys, as nice girls 'don't talk about it'.

My mum seemed very serious about sex, and she didn't smile once. She did fidget a lot, though—twisting and turning her wedding ring until I thought her finger might unscrew itself.

Anyway, when she was finished she said, 'Now, do you have any more questions?' By this stage she was standing over at the kitchen sink with her back to me, washing the dishes. I said no. And she was like, *Well, that's it, then. That's all you need to know. You can go now*. Thank God I had *Dolly*, and articles like how to tell if a boy was a good kisser, and what to do if a boy wanted to touch your boobs—and that kind of thing. That's what I really wanted to know. So, if I wanted to find out something about sex, I just consulted *Dolly*. It was kind of a relief not to have to ask Mum.

I wondered if I could get Mum to let me go to Becky's house after church. I didn't know if it was worth my while begging. I could tell her that Becky's mum would drive us home later, but Mum would say that meant she had to drive Becky home next time she came to our house, and we didn't have enough petrol money for that. I was convinced by now Becky would think I had deserted her. I guess I'd have to wait till school on Monday.

'Edwina!'

I looked up from the gravel to see a red Cortina pulled over on the side of the street. I squinted to see who it was. The occupant rolled the window down and rested his arm on the window sill.

'Edwina! Where's your old man?' he yelled from the car.

Oh, it was Tom. Tom Atkinson worked out in the vineyards with my dad.

'He's inside!' I yelled back, and pointed to the church.

'The hell I'm going in there! The place will fall down!' He laughed. 'Tell him I called past and that I've got his thermos, will you?'

'Okay.'

I had no idea how old Tom was—maybe twenty-something? He had dark receding hair, weathered suntanned skin and blue eyes. He and my dad knocked around a bit, and he came over to our house occasionally. They played in the same tennis team on Saturdays.

The engine revved and Tom turned back to the steering

wheel and swung the car around.

I looked back at the gravel and began to kick it again.

'Hey, Edwina!' Tom called out again. He didn't wait for an answer. 'Keep your knees together!' He let out a raucous laugh and, with that, he drove off.

I felt my cheeks turn warm. I stared curiously at Tom's car as it melted into the distance. Perhaps I gave him a few more seconds' thought and then shrugged him off. I even forgot to tell my dad that he'd called past.

CHAPTER 2

School Sucks. Or at least that was what was scribbled on the back of Kate Harold's school bag in black texta. My mum would have killed me if I'd drawn on my school bag. She thinks that kind of thing looks tacky.

I didn't actually think that school sucked that much—not that you'd admit it to anyone. It was at least one place where I got some space from my family.

Frau Wassarwitz (or 'Wobbly Tits', as the boys liked to call her behind her back) was our first period teacher. She was always late to class. When my dad had met Frau Wassarwitz at Parent-Teacher night last year, I overheard him say to Mum that she reminded him of women he'd seen in the foreign movies he watched around at Tom Atkinson's place. My mum walloped him with her handbag for that comment. I had no idea what he was talking about. She said that was fine for my dad to think like that—if he was into foreign accents and all that body hair. I tell you, some of the conversations my parents have go clean over my head.

When Frau Wobbly Tits finally arrived and let us into class, she asked us to all sit on the floor, as we were watching a documentary for health science class. She pulled the thick green curtains and started fiddling with the DVD player. At that point, I looked up and saw Becky standing in the doorway.

'Fraulein Cooper. You're late. That's a five-minute detention.'

Crap. Frau Wobbly Tits had to have been living on Mars not to have known what had happened in Becky's family in recent weeks.

Becky put her bag in the corner and came and sat down next to me. It was the first time I had seen her. She looked as if she'd been through the wringer. I took her hand and whispered, 'Are you okay?'

'Yeah, I can't wait to talk to you. Why haven't you called?'

'The evil witch of Wattleton was afraid I'd ring Child Protection Services if she let me near the phone.'

A weak smile crossed Becky's pretty freckled face. 'Can we go walking after school?' she asked hopefully.

Before I could answer, Wobbly Tits was on the warpath. 'Frauleins!' she shouted. 'You've just got a ten-minute detention! Stop talking!'

I whispered as quietly as I could, 'Sure Bec, I can't wait to talk to you either,' but Wobbly Tits had the radar ears that all teachers seem to have, and she bellowed, 'Fifteen minutes Fraulein Saltmarsh! Fraulein Cooper—zwanzig!'

I waited for Becky after school. Mum had already said I could walk home but I shouldn't go anywhere near the old football oval. Truthfully, I wasn't about to chance that either. The idea of walking anywhere near there gave me the creeps.

'God, she's loopy!' Becky said as we walked from detention. Thank God my mum wasn't picking me up from school—if she knew her daughter had been given a detention, I tell you she would have yelled at me so loud that people in small villages in Afghanistan would have known about it.

'Frau Wobbly Tits?'

'Yeah.'

With our school bags swung over our shoulders, we traipsed down the road, headed for the main street of Wattleton.

'So, Bec?' I asked, prompting her to take the lead. She looked at me with a pained expression and screwed up her nose. She shook her head, unable to find the words.

'You don't have to talk about it if you don't want to. I know it must be hard.'

'Anne-Marie has been throwing up,' Becky interrupted. 'She's lost a lot of weight.'

'Throwing up?' I didn't quite understand. What did that have to do with the attack? 'Has she got a stomach bug?'

I hated throwing up. The last time I puked had been about eight months ago when Dad cooked hot dogs for tea. He didn't realise they were five days past the use-by date. My mum said that was the last time Dad was setting foot in the kitchen. I'd hate to burst her bubble, but I think he was quietly happy with that.

'She's making herself do it,' Becky said. She quickly looked behind us to make sure no one was listening.

'I don't get it. How?'

'You stick your fingers into the back of your throat until you gag. You just keep doing it until you throw up. If you throw up everything you eat you can't get fat. You just get thinner.'

'God, that's completely gross! Does she want to be thin? I think I'd rather not eat.'

'Yeah, but you have to eat—you know, like in front of your parents at dinner. You can't get away with not eating all the time. They get suss. Anyway, I'm not sure it's because she wants to get thin. I think it's because of ...' Becky's voice drifted off.

I thought about it for a minute. 'Becky?'

'Yeah?'

'Is that how you're so thin?'

A quiet giggle escaped from Becky. Tossing her hair over her shoulders, she looked at me a moment still smiling, but the smile quickly faded. 'No, stupid. I'm just naturally like this.'

'So how do you know Anne-Marie's throwing up? Is she doing it, like, in front of you?'

'No. I walked in on her. I was busting to pee and she was crouched on the toilet floor holding her hair back and she had her fingers stuck down her throat. I thought she was choking on something at first, but then I realised she was making herself puke.'

'She told you that?'

'That she was puking? Yeah. I told her I'd tell Mum there was something wrong with her if she didn't tell me what she was doing.'

'So your parents don't know? You haven't told them?'

'Mum just thinks she's losing weight from the stress of what's happened—she hasn't eaten much at all since they released her from hospital. Mum says that she'll stop behaving like that soon, anyway. Mum reckons nobody can go on like that forever.'

'God. Has Anne-Marie said anything about ... you know?' I ventured.

'No. A counsellor lady from Backhurst came to the house, but she left her room two hours later saying Anne-Marie wouldn't talk to her. Can you believe it? After two hours? Dad said he wasn't paying her, but the lady said her services were free anyway.'

'Wow.'

'Yeah, you said it.' Bec adjusted her school bag with obvious effort. 'I can understand it being difficult to talk about, you know. If it had happened to me. Well ...'

'Have you tried to talk to her about it?'

'Sort of. I didn't really know how to. I mean, think about it, Ed. I didn't really talk to her before about boys and stuff. Reading her diary was the only way I found out about who she liked. If we didn't talk to each other about boys and sex then, well, it doesn't make it any easier now.'

'I suppose.' Thinking about it, I probably wouldn't want to talk about it if it happened to me. I couldn't think of anything worse than telling my mum something like that—or anyone in Wattleton for that matter. Can you imagine having to explain how someone did that to you? I could hardly talk to my mum about getting my period, let alone that.

'The counsellor lady spoke to us as a family and said Anne-Marie was probably feeling traumatised right now. She said she'd talk about it eventually—she just can't right now because she's still in shock.'

We crossed the street and headed past the retirement village where my nanna lives.

'Everyone's talking about it, Ed,' Becky said. It sounded like a statement, but I think she meant it as a question.

'No they're not,' I lied. What else could I do?

'You think?'

'Sure.' I looked the other way when I answered her.

'Do you think anyone thinks it was her fault?' Becky persisted. I immediately thought of my mum. *She was asking for it.*

'If they do, Bec, then they're idiots. Anne-Marie was walking home. She was attacked. She didn't even know the guy—right?'

'Right.' Becky sighed heavily, wearily trying to affirm in her own mind that people surely had to see that.

'So what else has been happening?' I said, to change the subject. 'I hear Kylie Baxter has the hots for Joey Parsons.'

'Yeah, there's a news flash.' A smirk crossed Becky's face. 'You know, Ed, before any of this happened, I was going to tell you something—something that happened before the rape ...'

'Tell me what?'

'I kissed Matty Rogers.' Normally Becky would have been bursting at the seams to tell me something like this, but today, well, the news just seemed kind of bland.

'So how did you guys end up kissing?'

'My dad invited his friends around after the pub and Matty came around with his dad.'

'Where was your mum?'

'At Lola's house, sewing quilts. And Anne-Marie was locked in her room studying like she always is ... was.'

'So where did it happen?' I asked.

'We went into my room and we were sitting on my bed and I was showing him some music I liked and next minute he just leaned over and started kissing me.'

I imagined Matty Rogers—pimply-faced Matty Rogers—sitting next to Becky, waiting for the right moment to attempt that first kiss. I imagined he'd move in as Becky leant back. Next, he'd cup her chin and stare into her eyes and passionately lock lips with her, just like they do on *Neighbours*.

'And Ed ...'

'What?'

'Promise you won't tell anyone?'

'Cross my heart and hope to die ...'

'He touched my ...' She pointed to her chest with a demure grin.

'You're kidding!'

'Na.'

'Were you embarrassed?'

'A bit—but then it kind of felt nice and then just normal, like he'd done it heaps of times before.'

'Did you touch him?'

'Of course not!' We both squealed laughing. The moment was short-lived. Seconds later I found myself feeling guilty—and Becky seemed to as well. Talking about such a thing seemed wrong somehow.

'I shouldn't have told you about it.' Becky went quiet for a moment, and then suddenly she picked up pace, her anger building. 'Anyway, that was then. All men are pigs now, as far as I'm concerned.'

I didn't know what to say. Were they? 'Oh Bec, do you really believe that?'

'Yes. No. I want to. I don't know. I'm not sure how to feel to be honest. Can we not talk about it?'

'Yeah, sure.'

When we reached the deli, Becky bought me a lollipop and we sat on the seat outside, chucking our bags beneath us. People moved to and fro past the store. Some faces I knew, some I didn't. Some passers-by stared at Becky with that *I'm so sorry* look. Some pretended not to notice her, but when they thought we weren't looking, they turned to take a second look. The unwanted attention made Becky uncomfortable.

'Have I grown a second head or what?' Becky asked angrily, ditching her lollipop on the footpath and heaving her school bag over her shoulder.

'Hi, Edwina.'

I looked up to see Tom walking past.

'Twice in one week—I'm lucky.' He walked into the deli.

'Who's that?' Becky asked.

'Some guy my father works with.'

'He's kind of cute,' Becky said, her eyes trailing after him.

'As if! He's ancient. He has to be, like, twenty-five,' I said. 'What makes you think that?'

'Dunno. He just is.'

I rolled my eyes at her. One minute all men were pigs, and the next she was checking out the local talent on my behalf.

Tom came out of the deli carrying an iced coffee and the newspaper. 'See ya, Edwina,' he said, smiling at me.

I looked down at the ground, my cheeks feeling hot again.

'All men *are* pigs,' Becky said, her nose high in the air as we watched Tom climbing into his car. I wondered if her sudden outburst had more to do with the fact Tom hadn't said hello to her.

CHAPTER 3

On Saturday, Mum was taking the family to the Wattleton Royal Show. Shows are pretty crap if you ask me. The cool rides that city kids get to go on never make it out here to the country.

Mum had entered every cake-cooking contest there was that day, so it was a real debacle even getting there. I got up reluctantly just before the crack of dawn to the tune of my mum's shrill screeches. I swear they were on a par with those of a soprano singer whose foot had been trodden on. Mum had opened the fridge to reveal that during the night, a cake-snaffling fiend had demolished half of her prized apple and walnut cake. George, Matthew and I had come out into the kitchen to see what all the noise was about.

'Who did this?' Mum screamed.

No one was talking.

'I don't have time for this!' She hurled the rest of the cake on to the kitchen bench, the plate spinning several times and stopping perilously close to the edge. Mum's interrogation skills were legend. I swear she'd make a packet if she worked for the FBI. 'One of you did this! Don't tell me someone broke into our house in the dead of night and stood at our fridge eating apple and walnut cake. It was one of you ... Who?'

'Well, your cake is pretty popular, Mary ...' I think this was my dad's attempt at humour. His comic timing needed some serious work. 'Maybe you can ice over it ... fill in the gaps with cream?' he offered.

Mum was ropeable. She narrowed her eyes and gave Dad a piercing stare. 'You think this is funny, Shaun?'

She started frantically shuffling food around in the fridge, placing the cakes one by one on the kitchen bench.

Dad let out a long sigh. 'No, Mary, I don't think—'

'Then why are you making fun of it? I was up until two a.m. icing those cakes, Shaun! Two a.m.!' she screamed, waving a stick of metwurst at him.

George and Matthew ran back to their room and slammed the door.

'Well, the damage is done, Mary. What's the use in getting stressed out about it?'

'You really don't get it, do you, Shaun?' Mum slammed the metwurst down on the bench, making the plates jump. She marched out of the room yelling, 'Quit standing there, Edwina—get dressed and help your brothers!'

The car ride to the show sucked with a capital S. We each had to hold a cake on our lap. Mum was driving because she said Dad couldn't be trusted not to find every pothole in the road on the way there. Dad held two cakes in Tupperware containers piled on top of one another—the carrot cake and the almond cake. He held them still, with his chin leaning on the top container. George had the chocolate fudge. My mum said if he even dared stick his finger under the cling wrap he could spend the rest of the day locked in the car. Matthew had the caramel cream roll and I had the apricot surprise. I couldn't work out what the surprise was, seeing that they had already told you there was apricot in it.

Turning into the showgrounds, Mum didn't see Reverend Lockhardt's enormous black four-wheel drive, and hit the brakes suddenly, throwing us forward in our seats. When we all halted, I quickly surveyed the car. Dad still had his two cakes; George had not laid a finger on the chocolate cake, and my apricot surprise was intact. Then I heard a long drawn-out wail from Matthew. The caramel cream roll had rolled onto the floor. Mum craned her neck over the seat to see it collecting hair and tiny bits of gravel from underfoot.

The next twenty minutes of us trying to find a car park were accompanied by Mum yelling at Matthew and Matthew sobbing hysterically. When we got out, Matthew's best pants were covered with cinnamon sugar and cream. Dad said it could have been worse, that we could be paying for Reverend Lockhardt's rear bumper and a new fender for our car. Mum just told him to go hide the caramel cream roll behind the nearest shrub.

After delivering the remainder of the cakes and seeing my mum turning on the sweetness and light with the CWA ladies, we were each handed five dollars and told to go have fun. Five dollars would buy me a Bertie Beetle show bag if I was lucky. Dad headed for the bar, even though it was just past nine in the morning.

Everyone in Wattleton and the surrounding district turned up for the Royal Show. It was a big gossip fest about who was doing what, when, and to whom. There was cattle judging and sheep shearing. There was wine-tasting, quilt displays and art and craft. Members of the Backgammon Club had matching purple T-shirts this year, with *GAMMON* on the front and *BACK* on the back. I tell you, these people are geniuses. There was the crappy school art contest where you could win a few dollars for the best artwork. My art teacher, Ms Landy, had entered three of my latest pieces. I was up against Kylie Baxter, who had traced a picture of a house and a tree. The competition was stiff—not.

I walked towards the merry-go-round—the meeting point Becky and I had decided on.

''Bout time, Eddie!' Becky shouted when she saw me. 'Where have you been?'

'Don't ask.'

She looked me over a minute, and shrugged. 'Well, it couldn't have been as bad as my morning.'

'I don't know. Did it involve cake?'

'What?'

'Never mind—what happened to you?'

'Anne-Marie.'

'Oh really—what now?'

'Let's go to the swings,' Becky said.

We headed for the playground just outside the showgrounds.

'Mum busted her.'

'How do you mean?'

'Well, there was this really weird smell coming from her bedroom cupboard last night, so Mum went searching through her stuff.'

'And?'

'She found a bucket in the back of the cupboard with vomit in it.'

'You're kidding!' I felt queasy.

'Na. Mum freaked out! There must have been like a whole day's worth of spew in there. She did her block at Anne-Marie and made her go out on the front lawn and hose out the bucket. The neighbours came out to see what all the fuss was about. Then Mum sat in her bedroom crying all night with the door locked, and Dad paced around the house chain-smoking.'

'God. What about Anne-Marie?'

'She just hid in her bedroom until this morning.'

'So what happened this morning?'

'Well, Dad decided to force-feed her cereal and milk for breakfast, and I kind of ended up wearing it.'

'She spat it at you?'

'Yeah, and at Dad. But he just kept shovelling it down her throat one spoonful after another. Now Mum and Dad are holding her captive in the lounge room so she doesn't go and puke it up again.'

'Jesus.'

'Yeah, you said it.'

Sitting on the swings in the playground, we twirled around sideways until the chain would twist no more. Then we let our feet off the ground and spun around until we were dizzy.

'So how much money have you got?' Becky asked.

'Five dollars.'

'I've got twenty. Know what else I've got?' Becky said, smiling. Looking around to see that no one could see, she reached into her coat pocket and pulled out a packet of cigarettes.

'Where did you get those?'

'Dad's ciggie carton.' Becky laughed. 'Want one?'

I thought about it: my mum running into me later that day. *Have you been smoking, Edwina Saltmarsh? My God, girl, you just never stop to think about how embarrassing you are to me, do you? Everyone in town will know and think I'm a terrible mother.* I could hear it now. I would be grounded indefinitely and one day after the authorities had called off the search party, I would emerge from a life in exile, old and grey.

'I don't know, Bec. I might pass today.'

Becky shrugged. 'Suit yourself.'

To tell you the truth, I think I bum suck when I smoke. When I did once, it kind of made me catch my breath. Not like Becky. She could suck it in and choof it out through her nose. Becky said I had to learn to really suck the smoke down instead of holding it in my mouth. I didn't know what the big deal was with people saying you could get addicted to smoking. I'm telling you, you can definitely stop after one. I mean, it tastes so gross for one thing. And who would want to do it forever anyway? We watched a video in health science class where some woman had gangrene and was missing half her leg. She'd smoked for like twenty years.

'So, have you seen that guy again lately?' Bec said, flicking the ash and taking another drag. I imagined half of Bec's leg missing and green muck dribbling from the gaping wound. 'Ed ... Earth to Ed?'

'Huh?' Bec's leg magically re-grew.

'Pay attention. That guy ...?'

'What guy?' Who was she talking about?

'That guy—the one who likes you?'

'Tom?' I said, as if she was mad. 'I told you, Bec, he's like ten years older than me. He's my father's workmate. That's just stupid.'

'I saw the way he looked at you.'

'What happened to *All men are pigs*?' I shot at her, twisting on my swing seat, winding myself up again.

There was a long pause before she answered.

'My mum says,' she began slowly, 'what that man did to Anne-Marie ... Well, she reckons not all men are like that. She said there are plenty of men out there who do respect women. Mind you ...' She stopped to giggle. 'My Aunt June was having coffee at our house when we had this discussion, and she said she was yet to find such a bloke. Mum told her to put a cork in it. Anyway, my point is, Mum reckons I'll still find the right boy one day, and so will Anne-Marie, at least if she eats.'

'Do you think Anne-Marie will want a boyfriend after ... after being raped?'

Becky's head swung round. She stared at me, surprised I had said it—the word that everyone replaced with a nicer term. 'The alleged assault' was one I'd heard. Like Anne-Marie had been belted on the nose once or twice. Becky shook her head and looked back down at the rock she had been rolling back and forward with the ball of her foot. She booted it across the playground and didn't answer me.

'Bec?'

'I thought we were talking about you and Tom,' Becky said finally. 'How come we end up talking about Anne-Marie all the time? I'm so sick of talking about her.'

'Well, there is no me and Tom, Becky,' I said in an equally annoyed tone of voice. 'And *you* started talking about Anne-Marie.'

Becky jumped off her seat and crushed her cigarette butt into the dirt. 'Stuff this. I'm going to see what Kylie Baxter's doing. See you later.'

'Bec!' I called after her, but I was caught in the swing. I let my feet off the ground, spinning and spinning. When I finally stopped, she'd disappeared.

Mum won first prize for her apricot surprise cake, which actually turned out to be surprising. Kylie Baxter won the art competition. One of my pieces came second. Kylie Baxter's mum was one of the judges, would you believe, which I hardly think was fair. I pointed this out to Mum, but she said it wasn't nice to suggest Kylie Baxter's mum was being unethical—whatever that's supposed to mean.

CHAPTER 4

Becky wouldn't speak to me at school. She wouldn't even look at me. She stood with Kylie Baxter and her friends, huddled in a little group outside the prefab before the bell had rung, and whispered loud enough for me to hear as I walked past, '*Tart*.'

I felt a queasiness stirring in the pit of my stomach. Unsure where to look or who to speak to, I stood quietly at the back of the line and kept my head down. Everyone was whispering and there were muffled fits of giggles. I lifted my gaze enough to see Kylie whispering something in Carly Tattler's ear, peering sideways at me over the hand that shielded her mouth. Carly was shaking her head with an expression of disgust on her face and glaring in my direction. I swallowed hard. I could feel my heart thumping and that horrible hot prickly feeling spreading all the way to my fingers and toes. It had to be about my argument with Becky. To be honest, I didn't think it was much of an argument at all. I *so* wished it had never happened. I had to learn to keep my mouth shut sometimes. Moments later I realised Carly was coming towards me. Oh God.

'Hi, Ed.'

'Hi, Carly.'

'So, Ed—have a good weekend?' Carly smiled sweetly at me. I looked towards Bec and Kylie, who were watching us from afar. Kylie clutched her school books and swayed with the rhythm of a metronome. She made me dizzy.

'Yeah—it was okay.'

'I heard you said something pretty bitchy about Anne-Marie to Becky.'

'Did you?' I attempted to be dismissive but I think the quiver in my voice gave me away. *Go away, Carly. Go away and find a mirror to distract yourself with.* The other kids in the line turned around to watch.

Carly looked knowingly at me.

'Did you hear Bec and Kylie and I are going to Joey Parsons' birthday next week?'

'No. I hadn't heard that.'

'Just thought you'd like to know.' Carly began to walk away, but she stopped for a moment and looked back at me over her shoulder, smiling. She returned to Kylie and they huddled together giggling.

At morning recess I faked a stomach ache. The receptionist believed me right off, because I was never sick. Never wanted to go home, more like it.

Mum didn't say much when she picked me up, except that I'd called her out right before *Dr Phil* was due to start.

I curled up on the couch and fretted about Becky and Kylie Baxter and Co. I sat through *Dr Phil.* Mum was throwing her arms up in disgust and cursing at the television. 'Can you believe the people they have on this show? If they only had Jesus in their lives,' she said as she paired socks from the washing basket.

At one o'clock, Mum said I could stay home while she drove Nanna to the doctor's. The very second her car had left the driveway, I rang Becky's house. The phone rang out. I tried a second time and still no answer. I wondered if there'd been another crisis with Anne-Marie. I wanted to leave a message with Becky's mum for Becky to call me. I knew she'd be different when Kylie and Carly weren't hanging around telling her what to say.

I went to my room and stood there for a moment thinking how best to use this moment when I was completely alone in the house. No screaming brothers breaking down my door. No mother bursting through my door to put folded washing in my drawer. No TV blaring from the next room, rattling my head senseless. I swung open my cupboard door and dragged the chair over from my desk. I stood on it so I could see my whole body in the mirror. I wished we had a full-length mirror like Becky did, not this stupid little square mirror stuck to the back of the cupboard door. I looked myself up and down and turned sideways, checking my profile. I pushed my nose up with my forefinger until it looked like Becky's. I was having plastic surgery one day, for sure. I swear to God, with my first earnings, I was going to get a nose like Becky's. I hated my nose. It wasn't bent or anything, and certainly had no obvious lumps. It just wasn't small and cute like hers.

I didn't hate everything about the way I looked. I liked my hair, for example. It was long and brown with a few natural blonde highlights. My dad insisted girls should have long hair, and so I had never had it cut short in my entire life. Dad used to plait it when I was little—there are photos of me with pigtails and ribbon. My dad stopped doing my hair when I was about ten or eleven years old. Come to think of it, that was probably when he stopped kissing and cuddling me too. *I'm not the touchy feely type, Ed*, he just started to say one day. He'd gently put me at arm's length and then pat me on the back. Mum said grown men sometimes get a bit nervous around little girls. I've never really understood what she meant by that.

I batted my eyes at the mirror. They were large and green, but my eyelashes weren't as curled as *Dolly* said they should be. And my freckled olive skin didn't have that healthy glow that *Dolly* said made you naturally beautiful. I wasn't butt ugly or anything I suppose. Not like Tara Kennedy, a girl in my homeroom class. Dad said she looked like she'd been abducted in the dark of night and beaten over the head with the ugly stick once or twice. Mum said Tara was just very 'unfortunate-looking', which my nanna said was polite terminology.

I chose a dance mix on my stereo and used my hairbrush as the microphone. I pretended I was a superstar on the stage with millions of fans cheering and applauding me. I dug out a long pink satin nightdress from my drawer that Becky and I used to play dress-ups with, and put it on, prancing around and shaking my backside at the mirror. I pushed my breasts up as if I was wearing a pushup bra. Thank God I had breasts. A girl in my class called Hayley Norman was constantly teased because she was a late developer. I felt a bit sorry for her. It would definitely suck if all the other girls had breasts before you did.

I found Nanna's white leather gloves, the ones with little pearls as buttons down the arm, and I piled on every cheap plastic bangle I could find in my jewellery box. I painted on some red lipstick and mascara. I pulled out a cigarette from my hiding spot in the space at the back of the sock drawer and pretended to smoke it, blowing fake smoke into the air and winking seductively at my reflection.

A loud thud startled me. Someone was banging on my bedroom window. I lunged for the stereo and managed to turn it off. I dropped the cigarette and kicked it under my bed. I swung round to look back at the mirror. There I was in my pink satin nightdress, my plastic bangles, and my bright red lipstick. The banging continued, but now there was a voice—a male voice.

'Hey—is anyone home?'

Through the thick lace curtains I could make out the silhouette of a man trying unsuccessfully to see inside. Those curtains were pretty heavy, and so I knew he couldn't see me, but he'd heard the music and knew someone was there.

'Hey! Mary—is that you?'

I recognised the voice—it was Tom, my dad's friend. I yelled back, 'No, it's Edwina!'

'Hey! I've been ringing the door bell. Can you open up?'

'Um ... okay.' Oh no. I didn't have time to change or scrub the make-up off my face. What the hell was he going to say?

I made my way out to the front door and opened it only slightly, peering around the crack, keeping my body behind the door. Tom leaned his head to the side, trying to see inside.

'Hi, Ed—is your mum home?'

'No, just me. She went out.'

Tom was wearing a blue and white check flannelette shirt

over a white singlet with jeans and sandshoes. His Levis were ripped, and discoloured from working in the vineyard. He ran his large calloused hands through his hair, scratched his head and then looked over his shoulder and down the road. Then he looked back at me inquisitively, with a slightly amused smile.

'What are you doing at home? Aren't you meant to be at school?'

'Um, yeah ... Well, I'm sick.'

'You don't look sick,' he said.

I didn't respond.

'What's with the make-up?'

Think quick, think quick ...

'There's a school play coming up, and I'm trying on my costume.' My creative ability under pressure astounded me.

'Oh, cool—can I see?' And with that, Tom put his foot in the door and forced it open with the strength of one muscular arm. I let go, unable to stop him.

I stood there while he looked me up and down, shaking his head slowly. Cupping his chin with his hand, he stroked his bristly stubble. My cheeks filled with the burning heat of humiliation. I fidgeted, folding my arms across my chest trying pointlessly to cover myself up, and then unfolding them again, clenching and unclenching my hands at my sides. I couldn't speak. What was I supposed to say? He obviously thought I looked like the biggest idiot on the face of the planet. It amazed me that he wasn't already doubled over with laughter. In fact, he wasn't saying or doing anything. He was just looking at me.

'I like it, Edwina. You look ... very sexy.'

Excuse me? What did he just say? Surely he didn't ... No. He had to be joking.

'I ... I ...' I couldn't look at him. I felt a cold wave of prickles enveloping my body and I couldn't breathe properly.

'You're shaking,' he said, in a noticeably quieter voice.

I found my voice. 'Oh, I'm just cold wearing this. I should go change.'

He stared at me for a minute, as if his blue eyes saw right through me. With a grin creeping across his face, he turned towards the door. 'Tell your mother I called around, will you?' He opened it and stepped outside. We resumed our positions, with me hiding modestly again. 'Tell her I'll catch up with your old man one night this week.'

'Okay, I will.'

'And Ed ...'

'Yeah?'

'Make sure you're wearing that when I come around.' He smiled and looked directly into my eyes. He held my gaze long after his smile had subsided and turned into a serious kind of look.

I closed the door. I didn't realise until I heard the engine start outside that my heart was pounding. I peered out the window. The car was still in the driveway, with the engine revving. Tom seemed to be looking right at the living room window as if he was contemplating something. Then he reversed out and was gone.

CHAPTER 5

Our annual church event, the Blessing of the Crops, was coming up. This is when we all get to stand around in hideous dark green velvet robes and sing stupid songs that would hopefully convince God to rain all over the local farm crops and vineyards. I think God has got way more important things to do like feeding starving children, which in my opinion He's not so hot at and He should focus a bit more on. Reverend Lockhardt would probably think that was a blasphemous thing to think, though Mum reckons he's eased up on the judgmental attitude since Mrs Lockhardt was booked for DUI. *Reverend Lockhardt—he's all about forgiveness now*, my mum said, like he wasn't before.

I sat at the front of the church with the adults, who stepped up to the pulpit one by one to present their allocated Bible reading. I didn't have to do a reading, thank Christ. I get really nervous when it comes to public speaking. Reverend Lockhardt said it was a huge honour to speak the words of Jesus and He gave him strength to stand and talk in front of a crowd. Obviously Jesus didn't make everyone feel the same, because the idea of talking in front of all those people just made me feel sick.

I don't pray very much, but I decided to say a quiet prayer about Becky. We hadn't spoken for what felt like an eternity. I asked God to help get Becky to talk to me and for God to give Anne-Marie her appetite back. I doubted God's to-do list for me was terribly big seeing I didn't pray too often. I figured He owed me for all the times I hadn't burdened Him with stuff to do. Last week Becky had been absent from school and I had overheard Kylie Baxter telling Carly Tattler that Anne-Marie had been admitted to the hospital after she had passed out at netball training. I also overheard Carly telling Kylie that she thought

Anne-Marie had faked her collapse. Can you believe it? These girls are so two-faced, I'm telling you. Anyway, I really wanted to tell Becky about Tom coming over and what he'd said about me being sexy. Maybe Becky had been right. Maybe she was, like, psychic or something. Maybe he really did like me. Becky would definitely be able to tell if he did. She knew how to find out stuff like that.

Sitting there in church, I thought about Tom. What did I really know about him? He played tennis with my dad. He worked in the vineyards. He drove an old red Cortina. That's all I knew. And he was older—like ten years older—at least. God, I was dreaming if I thought I had a chance with a guy like that, anyway. So what if he thought I looked sexy? That didn't mean he'd ask me out or anything. But a girl can dream, hey? And boy, did I dream, sitting there in that church pew ... about his blue eyes, about the smell of his black hair brushing my cheek, about him giving me my first ever kiss—and then how I'd brag my arse off at school. Then it occurred to me that God might know what I was thinking in church, and I really wanted Him to answer my prayer, and so I tried to stop thinking about Tom. I was surprised that was easier said than done.

My family had to stay after the morning service and attend choir practice. Reverend Lockhardt told all of God's Little Kingdom to sit quietly at the back while Cecile Campbell handed out ceremonial candles for each child to hold.

Someone must have realised that I didn't belong in God's Little Kingdom any longer. I guess that meant I now was a member of God's Big Kingdom, and I wondered if that was actually worse.

Matthew and George, wearing green robes with purple twisted cords tied around their waists, sat in the back row and giggled as they looped Robbie Cox's robe cord over the pew rail. Matthew put out the palm of his hand and George slapped it. Boys are so pathetic. I wished I was an only child. Better yet, I wished I was adopted.

Cecile Campbell approached the back row with a box full of candles. Encircling each candle was a piece of cardboard and the children were told to grip the candle below it. Cecile lit each candle with a cigarette lighter. I wondered if she secretly smoked, and that was why she had the lighter.

Cecile warned the children to hold the candle still and upright, so that any dripping wax would theoretically land on the cardboard and not on their hands. Of course, as soon as Cecile's back was turned, God's Little Kingdom became God's Little Fire Brigade, and they each took turns running a finger through the naked flame, blowing it out and reigniting it again with another candle.

In such a situation, as sure as God made eggs, you could count on my brothers to top the class in the ingenuity stakes. Matthew gave George a wonderful idea. Why don't they burn the cardboard? Just singe it a bit and brown off the edge? So Matthew held his candle and George graciously held his candle's flame to the edge of Matthew's cardboard, and together they carefully burned the edge. This worked for a while, and Matthew successfully burned the entire circumference of his candle holder. But when George attempted the same, his lit up, crackling and burning quickly up the side. Matthew frantically tried to blow it out, but that only fanned the flame.

Suddenly George leapt from his seat, the candle holder now well and truly alight. Not knowing what to do, he ran down the aisle to the front of the church, hoping one of the adults could extinguish it.

Not a moment too soon, the flame bit at his fingers, and he let out a loud yelp. He dropped the candle, immediately setting fire to the carpet. It spread until the flames curled and leapt at the foot of the altar. Horrified, the adults didn't seem to know what had hit them. They sat motionless for a few seconds, watching the flames.

'Good God, George!' Mum squealed, standing up. 'What the hell are you doing?'

George, now in tears and hopping up and down squeezing his hand in pain, backed away from the small bonfire. Running to the back of the church, he huddled next to a rather shocked and pale-looking Matthew. The rest of God's Little Kingdom made a speedy exit out the back door, except for little Robbie Cox, who stood up and then fell flat on his face behind a pew.

The fire took off, dissolving the old red carpet, and gave off a horrible thick black smoke that quickly filled the room. Margaret Taper began coughing and thumping her chest with her fist, fanning the smoke that swirled around her.

As the congregation recovered from its collective shock, the church elders lurched forward and started stomping on the flames with their very best church-going shoes.

Reverend Lockhardt saved the day by throwing the flask of communion water on the fire, quashing a fiery path that had already eaten a hole larger than a hula hoop in the carpet.

The smoke silently dispersed and everyone slowly turned to stare at Mum's face, which was surely whiter than the Holy Ghost. She drew a limp hand up to her mouth and blinked several times as if her eyes had deceived her. A tiny squeak from the back of her throat was the only noise audible in a room where you could have heard a pin drop.

My mum's worst nightmares had come at once. Public humiliation in my mum's world seemed a sad, unfortunate, yet inevitable fact of life.

CHAPTER 6

'So I hear your brothers are considering a career in arson,' Becky said when she called me Sunday night. That was it—no *Sorry I haven't spoken to you for weeks*. Just straight back to normal like nothing happened. She wasn't one for saying sorry. But that was Becky, take it or leave it. And I decided it was better to take it.

'Yeah, you should have heard my mum when we got home,' I whispered, taking the handset to my bedroom.

'I bet she went sick at you lot.'

'Well, not me for once.'

'So I guess you know I've been away from school?' Becky sighed.

'Yeah.'

'Have you heard Anne-Marie is in hospital?'

'I heard Kylie and Carly saying something about it.'

'Yeah,' Bec said cautiously, avoiding the topic of Kylie and Carly, and added, 'They're feeding Anne-Marie through a tube now.'

'They're what?' I imagined a thick see-through plastic tube wedged in Anne-Marie's mouth, with bits of apple, hot dogs, and Tim Tams flying up it.

'They have a drip in her arm—to feed her nutrients into her blood.'

Oh. 'Is it working?'

'Sort of, I think. They've had to sedate her, too. She tried to rip the tube out a couple of times. You can't talk to her after the injection. It's like ... She's like ... not there ...'

I didn't know what to say.

'So what's new with you?' Becky asked.

'Um ... Well, you know what you said about Tom ... I think ... Well, I can't be sure—but I think he might actually like me.'

'I told you so!' Becky squealed. I mouthed it along with her. I knew she'd say it. 'So what are you going to do about it?'

'I don't know, Bec. How can I find out if he really does?'

'Flirt. You have to flirt.'

'How?'

'I don't know ... Just, like, smile at him and stuff—let him know you're there.'

'I don't even know when I'm going to see him again. It's not like he comes around regularly.'

'Well, when he does, make sure you make him notice you,' Bec said. 'Damn, I have to go. Mum's going nuts at Aunt June for putting cutlery in the microwave again. Let me know how it goes.'

Tom was in the family room chucking back tinnies with my father. I stayed in my bedroom, even though Mum had asked me to come out and say hello to *our company*. I love how she uses words like that when other people are around to hear them. Anyway, I was the hugest chicken on the planet—like I was going to go out there and flirt with Tom like Becky said to—be real!

I was doing my art homework. My class had to create portraits this term and I was finishing one of my dad. I was using charcoal. Horrible stuff—my hands were blackened and it was under my fingernails. Mum had had a fit when she'd seen it. 'You get that on your doona cover, Edwina, and you can forget about Becky's house for the next month.' I was extra careful not to touch anything other than the paper.

Mum said I'd never make a living from my art. She said there were heaps of artists out of work and they all had crappy day-jobs like working in cafés to support themselves, because paintings and sculptures don't pay you squat until you're dead—and then art becomes worth something. She said all the great artists are dead and no one knows the names of the living artists anyway. She thinks I should be a secretary or a bank clerk, because they're safe, decent jobs and you know where your next pay cheque is coming from. I never heard my art teacher Ms Landy say anything like this. Ms Landy is an art teacher and she has a job, doesn't she?

I smudged in the shadow of my dad's cheeks, and left some of the white paper untouched to create the light in his eyes. I shaded the hollow below his eyebrows to just the right depth, and created flecks in his hair that looked like the strands of greys I had noticed developing around his ears.

I had contemplated going to the family room. I hadn't been able to stop thinking of Tom and the comments he'd made and whatever it was that had happened between us. That word 'sexy' played over and over again in my head, and the strange way he had looked at me. It was as if he was trying to let me know he liked me. How could I be sure he was actually flirting with me? It was such a strange concept to me that someone of his age was interested in someone as young as me. I had to be dreaming.

But God, he was so good-looking, with his dark hair and sun-kissed skin. I wasn't used to considering the way an older man looked—it had never struck me to consider looking before. It was almost madness to find myself even thinking about him in this way. I mean, he was a friend of my father's! Not just some guy from school. He hung out with my father. Worked with him. Played tennis with him. Drank beer with him. Talked footy with him. What was Tom going to do—talk about me with my dad? *So Tom, been out on any hot dates lately? Yeah Shaun, your daughter is a real hottie—I'd like to ask her out if that's okay with you.* As if!

Even though I was pretty taken aback at the time, there was something very real about the way he had spoken to me. He seemed to mean it when he said I looked sexy. Something inside was telling me to go out there. What harm could it do if I flirted with him a bit? If he actually did like me, I should be able to tell. Maybe I should dress up again, to get his attention. He said he wanted me to wear that pink slip. God. I couldn't do that. Mum would wonder what the hell I was up to.

I found my white lacy crochet top that cut just above my midriff. I teamed that with a red mini skirt and white lace-up boots. I scrunched my hair so it fell tousled on my shoulders and I put on some black eyeliner to create that smoky effect that *Dolly* said was really hot this season. I evaluated my reflection. I liked what I saw. If he was into looking—he would look at this. No question.

I felt my heartbeat quicken as I left the room. Showtime.

My mum's eyes widened as she saw me. 'Why are you dressed like that, Edwina?'

'No reason. I felt like making an effort,' I said. I wished she hadn't drawn so much attention to the fact I looked different—like this wasn't the norm after school every night.

Mum raised her eyebrows but didn't comment further. I had banked on the fact she wouldn't create a scene in front of company. I knew that I'd probably get a lecture later tonight on dressing like a lady. She excused herself to go cook the dinner. That left my dad, Tom and I. My brothers were playing in their bedroom and had been ever since they got home from school.

My dad slurped down the last mouthful of his beer and put his hand out for Tom's empty can. Without saying a word, he went to get another round of beers from the fridge.

Moving from the doorway, I walked over and casually sank into the softness of the couch and gazed straight at the television, pretending not to even really notice Tom. I could feel him looking sideways at me. I crossed my legs and twirled a strand of hair around my finger.

'Hi Ed.' Tom's voice was quiet, barely heard over the blare of the television.

'Oh hi,' I said, doing my best to sound unimpressed.

There was silence as we watched the Diet Coke ad on TV.

'Where's your pink dress?' was the next thing Tom said. I swallowed hard to conceal my shock, but when I looked at him he was smiling. He jabbed my side with his finger. I jumped. He did it again, and this time he was tickling me.

'Cut it out!' I laughed. But I hoped he wouldn't.

'Why don't you wear the pink dress?' he taunted, tickling me again. His hands were now on both sides of me—digging into my ribs. I squirmed around, my mini skirt riding my thighs, my midriff top climbing higher and higher.

'What you have on is okay, anyway. I s'pose,' he said, stopping and sitting back, his eyes trained on my legs.

'You think so?' I asked, holding my breath.

Tom glanced towards the door and then slid closer to me on the couch. 'Yeah. I really like that top you've got on.' My heart skipped a beat. 'I like your skirt, too.' He lightly trailed a finger up the outside of my thigh. I felt my skin tingle. He had moved in so fast and unexpectedly it made me dizzy.

'Here we go, Tom, one brewed just the way you like it, buddy!' my dad announced enthusiastically on returning to the room. He thrust a tinnie into Tom's hand. 'So who do you reckon will go down this week—the Roosters?'

'Oh yeah—they've got no hope,' Tom chuckled, but he was still looking at me.

My dad didn't notice that Tom had moved closer to me. Hot prickles ravaged me in anticipation my dad would notice that Tom's hand had slipped quietly between us and glided just under my knee. My dad was too engrossed in the footy, and I noticed Tom kept glancing at my dad with each stroke of his hand. I knew then it was a secret between us, and I was to play along.

At first it was as light as a tickle, with only one finger, and then it was a firmer, more deliberate stroke with his whole hand, running up and down my leg. I lifted my leg ever so slightly, and his hand was underneath, moving as close as he could to my backside and trailing down to just under my knee. He kept his eyes on my dad the whole time, stopping only to add to the conversation, chuck back another mouthful of beer and to run his hands through his hair.

'Ed, why are you watching footy? Haven't you got homework to do?' Dad asked, as if he had only just realised I was sitting there.

Tom suddenly clasped his hands behind his head, and seemed to be massaging his neck. He seemed almost nervous for a minute, and then he turned to me and said, 'Getting out of your homework, huh?'

'Yeah,' I said, standing up. Truthfully though, I didn't want to go anywhere.

I went back to my room. Tom's eyes followed me out the door. Sitting on my bed, I thought I would surely keel over and die of shock. I was consumed with thinking about Tom, what had just happened and what it meant. God—he really *did* like me! I couldn't believe a guy that much older was interested in me! Me! I wasn't even the most popular girl in school. I wasn't captain of the netball team. I didn't do anything that made me noticeable. Why me? Why not Kylie Baxter—little Miss Popularity? Why not Becky, with her beautiful hair and cute button nose?

My mind began to wander. What would it be like to kiss him? I hadn't even kissed a boy—ever. Well, not counting that quicker-than-a-microsecond kiss on the cheek I got from Albert Heath in the fifth grade. I bet Tom kissed really well. I bet he really did kiss like they did on *Neighbours*—all open mouthed, with their eyes closed and making those panting sounds. Maybe he had fallen in love with me already? Maybe he knew that from the first time he ever saw me and that's why he's been giving me those looks every time he passes me in the street. Wow! What would it be like to be in love with an older guy? He had a car! Snot that, Kylie Baxter! What are you going to do? Ride home on the back of some high school boy's pushbike?

I didn't even know what love felt like. How would I know if I was in love? Did he love me? If he did love me, I bet he'd bring me flowers or gifts. All the loved-up guys in the movies bring gifts. They also give Valentine's cards and even perfume. Maybe he'd take me on romantic dates to lookouts and fancy restaurants. We could go on long walks through the vineyards and sit on the veranda and watch the sunset. Wow! How cool would it be if we were in love?

Maybe Tom thought I was older, though. Maybe he didn't realise I was fourteen. Did I look older? Maybe dressing like this made me look older. I wished I was older. God, there were a lot of maybes. Not to mention the big fat maybe-I'm-dreaming maybe.

I looked up to see Tom quietly closing my bedroom door behind him. He put a finger to his lips. 'Shh—I'm supposed to be in the loo.'

I couldn't hide the grin that crept over my face. He walked over to my bedside, his hands plunged in his pockets. He leant over my shoulder, looking at my artwork. 'That's your father,' he said.

'Yeah.' There he was, in my room, alone with me. The silence was thick, and something unsaid was definitely going on between us.

'It's very good.' He pulled a hand from his pocket and trailed his finger over my drawing. 'I like the way you've drawn his lips—like he is about to say something ...'

'Thanks,' was the only response I could think of.

His finger glided slowly from my drawing and up to meet my cheek, where he drew a strand of hair that hung over my face and tucked it behind my ear. Warm prickles flowed through my body. I shuddered with the anticipation of what he would do next.

'Stand up, Ed,' he whispered. I did, as if I was obeying a command.

'I like you, Ed ... you know ... Do you understand?' He was standing inches from me. The smell of his deodorant wafted gently through the air. His large frame dwarfed me as I looked up at his face. 'I want to ... Well, you *make* me want to ... to kiss you ... I'm going to kiss you, Ed.'

I make him want to kiss me? Breathing was suddenly difficult. I nodded.

'This will be our secret,' he said, grasping my arms with his strong hands. He looked directly into my eyes. 'You can't tell anyone—okay?'

'Okay,' I said.

Why not? Why can't I tell anyone? I didn't think anyone would believe me, anyway. That this older guy wanted to kiss me—plain old Edwina Saltmarsh. It would be so cool to brag, to tell the other girls that this guy sneaked into my room when my parents weren't looking and kissed me. But if he said it was a secret ... Well, I just wanted him to kiss me so badly, so badly I ached. Maybe I wanted this to happen, not even for his kiss, but because this whole thing was so dizzy and exhilarating. It was the kind of thing that never happened to girls like me. I wouldn't tell—I'd never tell. Not a soul—not even Becky. Just so he'd kiss me and I could find out what it was like. My God, this had to be some kind of dream.

His hands firmly grasped my shoulders and he leant in to kiss me. Please let me kiss him right. Don't let him think I'm some stupid little girl who can't kiss. Please let him like me. No one like this had ever given me the time of day. Please let me get this right ...

His lips met mine. They weren't soft as I'd imagined, for a first kiss—they pressed firmly, almost desperately, down on mine. I let him kiss me, not really kissing back, not the way I'd practised with my dolls or my pillow when I was alone at night and had imagined a moment like this a thousand times over before drifting to sleep. I just let him kiss me and kiss me, again and again. His breathing was rapid and he pressed the whole of his body against mine. I closed my eyes and counted my blessings that this was happening—for real. It was so wonderful, so beautiful and so frightening all at the same time. Was this love? Was this what love was like?

He stopped abruptly and I was shaken back to reality. I opened my eyes as if awoken from some incredible dream.

'I should go,' he said, pulling away from me. Before I could ask him if I'd done something wrong, he was standing by my bedroom door with his hand on the doorknob. Looking back at me and as if realising my panic, he said, 'I liked that, Ed. I hope we get to do it again.'

'I do, too,' I said quietly.

Obviously, it wasn't something I'd done. It seemed a strange way to end such a moment.

His serious gaze turned into a smile. 'Remember,' he said, bringing his finger back to his lips, 'don't tell anyone, okay?'

'I won't.'

He left. I stood there, still tasting him on my lips. If that could happen again—I definitely wouldn't tell a soul. I wouldn't say a word. Not a single word to anyone. Not even to Becky. Not as long as I lived. Loose lips sink ships. That's what my mum says. And my ship was about to set sail.

CHAPTER 7

I got a C+ for my maths test. Mr Habermeil handed it back and shook his head, saying, 'Very disappointing, Miss Saltmarsh. Life as a farmer's wife is calling you.'

I hadn't been able to concentrate during the test. I kept thinking about Tom. I couldn't study without my mind wandering back to the secret that I had kept now for two weeks. Two weeks without a word to anyone. Two weeks of lamb chops and school, school and lamb chops, and nothing much in between.

I couldn't believe he hadn't called past our house or something. Maybe he didn't like me any more. Maybe he realised straight after kissing me that I was a terrible kisser and had no idea what I was doing. What if I had bad breath? My God, I forgot to check before he kissed me! *Dolly* says you should suck on breath mints before you kiss a boy. It also said to avoid eating garlic. Mum used garlic in all her cooking—and we're not even Italian! Ew! What if Tom thought I stunk like garlic? Did I?

After doing a breath check at lunch, I turfed my ham sandwich in the nearest bin and headed for the canteen. I didn't know if ham had garlic in it, but I decided it was better to play it safe. I had sneaked some money from Mum's purse before leaving for school. I could live with the guilt. We never got lunch money. I had to make sure that George and Matthew didn't see me.

I bought a chocolate ice-cream and headed for the school oval. A couple of kids saw me and I felt validated. I could go to the canteen too, just like any other kid in this school.

I found Becky sitting on the fence of the oval with a girl from a grade above us. Her name was Mardie Simpson. I knew a bit about her. It's a wonder anything could be kept a secret in this town. The grapevine worked so fine my dad said he should slap a patent on it and watch it bankroll.

Mardie Simpson had blonde hair and she was pretty. She had an older boyfriend who was from out of town. Someone said her mother was addicted to prescription drugs. I didn't really know what that meant. I pictured the antibiotics my mum got from the chemist and wondered why anyone would want to swallow those massive capsule things all day, and what the hell they did for you that was so wonderful, apart from making you nearly choke to death.

'Hey, Ed,' Becky said, 'this is Mardie.'

'Hi,' I said, cautiously slipping a leg over the fence rail. Damn. I dripped chocolate ice-cream on my school dress. I'd have to rinse it under the tap before I went home or Mum would notice it.

'Hi, Edwina,' Mardie said with a wide smile.

'Oh, that's okay. No one calls me Edwina—well, except my mother. You can call me Ed.' I slurped on my ice-cream.

'I'd prefer Eddie rather than Ed,' Mardie said.

'You can call me that too.'

'Okay.'

'Okay,' I said.

Mardie turned to Becky. 'Are you sure she's up for this?'

I love it when people talk like you're not even there. 'Yeah, Mardie. I told you, it's cool.'

'What's cool?' I said.

Mardie glanced at Becky.

Becky nodded.

'We're going to do some weed after school,' Mardie said.

'Oh, okay.' I had no idea what she was talking about.

Mardie took a deep breath and looked at Becky again.

'It's okay, Mardie. Ed smokes.'

Oh, smoking. She meant smoking. 'Cool,' I said, even though I didn't like smoking so much.

Mardie raised her eyebrows. 'Hayley Norman is coming too.'

'Hayley? As in the *Simpson Desert* Hayley?' I said, laughing.

Mardie looked at me like I was nuts. Becky came to my rescue. 'She means the lack thereof in the chest department. You know, Hayley doesn't have any bras yet. Barren, like the Simpson Desert.'

There was a heavy pause.

Mardie appeared unimpressed. 'She's my friend. And she's okay,' Mardie said, looking at me distastefully.

'Oh yeah, I'm sure she is.' *I should quit while I'm ahead*, I thought.

'I've gotta go. I'll see you at the gates after school.' Mardie got up and left.

I turned to Becky. 'I don't think she likes me.'

'Na, Mardie's okay. Doesn't like bitchy comments behind people's backs—you know? So, can you make it?'

I thought about it for a minute. Yeah, I could. I'd make up some excuse. 'So we're meeting for a smoke?' I asked.

'Some pot, Ed. We're going to smoke pot. You know—grass, weed? You smoke it,' Becky said with a deadpan expression.

Oh! They'd been talking about pot! I hadn't heard it called 'weed' before—well I guess that made sense. 'Oh my God, Bec! If we're doing it straight after school, are you sure my mum won't bust me?'

'Na. Your mum is so naïve. She won't have a clue.'

'Do you think I'll have time to, like, sober up?' My mum was a lot of things, but she wasn't entirely stupid.

'Honey—your mum wouldn't recognise if you were stoned. You just tell her you had a great day and you're in a good mood or something.'

I swear if they offered university degrees in lying, Becky would receive an honorary doctorate.

'Okay.' I guess I could act the part. No one suspected a thing about the kiss with Tom, and he had told me to keep that a secret. I could get away with the smoking pot thing, I suppose.

The bell rang. We headed back to class.

'What about the smell?'

'*This'll take care of it!*' Becky said, waving around a can of deodorant from her backpack.

That afternoon I forgot about Tom. I was consumed with the worry of smoking pot and my parents finding out. But if I backed out, Mardie would rag on me for being chicken. I guess Becky was doing it. She didn't seem worried. If Becky was okay about it, maybe it wasn't such a big deal. I guess I was about to find out.

Becky and I made our way to the main gates after the home time bell rang. I found Matthew and told him to tell Mum that I had an art project and I'd be late. I often stayed back to do my art, so I figured she'd swallow the story if I didn't take too long.

Mardie and Hayley were at the gates. Hayley didn't speak to me. She just smiled and said hello to Becky instead. We headed for the toilets near the church on the hill.

'So have you got a pipe?' Becky said.

'Sort of.' Mardie laughed.

'Mardie,' Hayley whined, 'we're not going to use a Coke can again!'

Again? So flat-chest Hayley was into pot. Interesting. Unexpected. Did smoking pot stunt your boob growth? I could swear I heard smoking anything can stunt your growth. I made a mental note to consult *Dolly* when I got home.

'No. Bill showed me a trick,' Mardie said. Bill was Mardie's boyfriend. 'We're going to use a carrot.'

'A what?' Becky said, stopping in the middle of the footpath and looking incredulously at Mardie.

'A carrot,' I said. 'I think she said *a carrot*.'

Mardie just looked at me for a moment as if trying to work me out. 'Yeah. I said a carrot.' We all kept walking.

'How the hell do you use a carrot?' Hayley asked.

'I've got one I prepared earlier,' Mardie said, laughing. She reached into her bag and pulled out her lunch box. Opening the lid, she took out a carrot that had the thin end of it cut off. It was carefully wrapped in cling wrap.

'Christ, Mardie! Put it away! Someone will see you!' Hayley said.

'Oh yeah? What are they going to do—arrest me for eating a carrot?'

She had a point.

We'd reached the toilets and went inside. I don't think anyone saw us. It was dim in there. The toilets were small and really dirty with graffiti on the walls. Mostly tags. If you wrote anything on the wall in Wattleton, chances are people would figure out who wrote it. Most of the toilet seats were cracked and hanging only by a hinge. The door locks were all busted and nobody had refilled the toilet paper in years.

'So Bill showed you this?' Becky asked.

'Yeah.' Mardie pulled out all her school books and dumped them on the concrete floor. She pulled up the hard cardboard bottom of her sports bag and took out a tiny plastic bag with hashed up grass in it.

'Is that how he smokes pot?' I asked. 'Through a carrot?'

Mardie smirked. 'Yeah, because of the health benefits.' She broke into a fit of giggles.

We all stood and watched as Mardie packed the cone-shaped hole of the carrot with the weed, squashing it in with her perfectly manicured nail. She pulled out a cut-off drinking straw from her school bag and wedged it into the hole on the side of the carrot.

'Ready, girls?' Mardie said, flicking her lighter. She held the flame over the weed until it took, sending the sweet smell through the toilet. She drew back on the straw and blew smoke out through her nose. She took a deep breath and coughed, passing the carrot to Becky. Becky looked at me and smiled. I smiled back. This was kind of fun. Becky took a drag and tossed her head back, blowing smoke. She passed the carrot to me.

I looked up at Mardie, who had a warm smile as she nodded at me to go ahead. I brought the straw to my lips and, holding the lighter over the top of the carrot, I drew in the heady smoke of the weed. I held it in until my head felt light and then blew out, passing the carrot to Hayley.

We all watched Hayley do the same.

We sat on the floor of the grotty toilet block passing the carrot pipe around. I didn't feel really bizarre, not like I expected to. That was apparently because the weed didn't have much 'head' in it, which Mardie said was the stronger stuff. I had no idea what she meant.

Mardie talked about her boyfriend Bill and how one of his mates called Sam kept coming over when Bill wasn't around. She said Sam had tried to crack on to her, but it didn't get further than a kiss. She reckoned Bill would string Sam up by his nether-regions if he found out. I hoped she wasn't for real—it sounded painful. Hayley told Mardie she'd take Sam off her hands if she wanted. She thought he was cute. I privately wondered if Sam would think the same about Hayley and her pancake breasts.

Not to be left out of the conversation on boys, Becky told the group about Matty Rogers, and how she had made out with him in her bedroom. The group then turned and looked expectantly at me. Becky burst out laughing and slapped me on the back. 'Ed hasn't kissed anyone yet,' she said, laughing as if she had just told the most hilarious joke on the planet.

'I have so!' I retorted angrily.

Becky stopped laughing immediately. She stopped so abruptly, it was like someone had flicked her on/off switch. She looked at me blankly. 'When? Who?' she said, passing the carrot to Mardie. 'Why haven't you told me?'

I shrugged. Perhaps it was the pot that was relaxing my entire body, or because Tom hadn't called or even come by our house since he had kissed me. Maybe I just wanted to be like one of the other girls. Perhaps I was sick of keeping the secret. What good is a secret unless you tell someone? 'Tom Atkinson. A couple of weeks ago,' I said, looking sheepishly at Becky.

Becky shrieked. I thought she'd kill me for not having told

her sooner, but instead she threw her arms around for me and cried out, 'Oh my God! I told you! What did I tell you? What did I tell you? He likes you!'

Mardie and Hayley looked at each other. Mardie asked, 'Who are you talking about?'

'Oh, just this guy. You probably wouldn't know him. He doesn't go to school,' I said proudly. My confidence seemed to shoot high into the air and do loops around the sun. *I had kissed a guy. I had kissed a guy*, I chanted in my head. No longer did I have to sit on the sidelines listening to the other girls brag. Now it was my turn, front and centre. The spotlight was on me. And an older guy—one who had a car.

'Maybe Bill knows him,' Mardie said, passing the carrot to Hayley.

'I doubt it,' I said coolly.

Hayley took a long drag. I couldn't believe what I saw next. The straw lit up like a neon light! Hayley dropped the carrot on the floor and slapped her hand over her mouth. Mardie rolled over backwards clutching her stomach, whooping with laugher.

'My lips!' Hayley cried out. 'I burned my lips!'

None of us could stop laughing. I was laughing so hard I was going to pee. I ran into a toilet cubicle and squatted over the seat. I came out and saw Becky examining Hayley's lips.

'They look okay, Hales. A bit red, maybe ...' Becky cupped Hayley's face in her hands. She burst into a fit of giggles again. 'Oh my God—I think there's a blister. Mardie—look at this—she's got a blister!'

Mardie examined Hayley's mouth. We crowded over Hayley viewing the tiny blister on the inside of her bottom lip.

I noticed Becky's eyes. 'God, Becky—your eyes are red!'

'So are yours!' she said. 'Anyone got a mirror?'

Mardie pulled out a make-up mirror from her school bag. We took turns looking. I wished I hadn't. My eyes were really red. Mardie handed us some eye drops. Becky squirted some into my eyes for me.

'We'd better get going,' Mardie said, packing her school books back into her bag.

'What about the carrot?' Becky said.

Mardie picked it up and threw it in the toilet.

'Gross!' Hayley laughed. 'There's always carrot bits!'

Mardie and Hayley left together, headed for Mardie's house. Becky and I inspected one another's bloodshot eyes again. She said she didn't think anyone would notice. Becky was used to that. No one noticed Becky in Becky's house any more—they only noticed Anne-Marie.

'Why didn't you tell me about Tom?' Becky asked, as soon as Mardie and Hayley were out of earshot. She stumbled and looked back to see what had caught her shoe. I'm telling you, there was nothing there. She linked her arm through my arm and pressed her body into mine. We started walking sideways.

'I don't know, Bec,' I said, shoving her back the other way. 'He made me swear not to tell anyone.'

'Why?' Becky giggled so hard, she was dribbling. 'Is he ashamed of you?' she added, wiping her chin.

I felt as if she'd taken thirty tonnes of bricks and dumped them on my heart. Could he be? Was he ashamed of me? I hadn't thought of that.

Suddenly it occurred to me that Becky might be jealous. We spent so much time talking about her and what she did with boys that maybe she didn't know how to handle the idea that I'd left the starting block.

We sprayed ourselves with deodorant and said our good-byes. I swung my school bag over my back so hard it just about caught me from behind and sent me flying. I started to walk home, confident I wasn't running late enough to warrant my mum's suspicions. I decided Becky *was* jealous. Tom did like me. Becky had heaps of boys who liked her, but for once this one liked me. For once, this one was mine.

CHAPTER 8

I headed up the road alone. Everything seemed a bit wobbly. My school bag felt like it weighed a tonne. The sun glared and I squinted, unable to see more than several metres in front of me. Suddenly I had this insatiable craving for corn chips. I really felt like just parking myself right there on the side of the road and hoeing into a bag of corn chips. I was so lost in my food fantasy, I failed to hear the car engine behind me. I barely heard the honking.

'Hey, Ed! What are you doing?' It was Tom. I leaned into the car window.

I tried to say, 'And where the hell have you been in the last two weeks?' but I think it came out kind of different. I fumbled with the door lock and smiled at him casually.

Tom stared at me for some time as if evaluating my condition. 'You're stoned,' he said finally.

'No I'm not.'

'You are so! Christ, Eddie, you'd better get in. If your mother sees you like that, we'll be scraping you off the ceiling in little pieces.'

I climbed in. He had grey lambswool seat covers. They felt soft against my bare legs. I swung my bag on to the back seat. We sat on the side of the road.

'Well, what are we going to tell your parents?' Tom asked, tapping his hands on the steering wheel. 'You can't go home like that for at least another couple of hours. They'll know something isn't right.'

'I don't know.' I was fiddling with his glovebox, rummaging through the contents. A tape, a tube of some kind of sunburn cream, some chemist scripts, a bottle opener. No corn chips.

'God. You owe me. You *so* owe me.' Owed him what? I briefly wondered. Tom pulled away from the side of the road and swung the car around.

I looked out the window. The trees seemed awfully tall today. They towered over us like skyscrapers, casting long shadows over the car. I leaned my head over until I was kind of looking at them upside down. They slowly whirled past me, their branches swirling like a thick green industrial paint against the blue sky.

'Stay here.' Tom said, getting out of the car. We'd stopped. Strange. How did we get to my house so fast?

'Tom, what are you doing?'

'Stay there and shut up.' Tom slammed the car door.

I slumped down and ran my hands through the warm wool of the seat cover, scooping the soft short fibres between my fingers. I turned and rubbed my cheek against it—it felt nice. I gazed out the window at Tom, who was standing on the front porch talking to someone through the screen door. I had no idea who. Seconds later, he was back in the car and we were driving up the road.

'What did you say?'

'I said you were coming out to my farm to help pick fruit. I said we'd bring back a few buckets for your mum. She reckons she can make jam.'

'Is that where we're going? To your farm?'

'Well, you might as well. It's going to take a few hours for that to wear off.' Tom laughed. 'You totally owe me, Ed. Your parents would bust your chops for smoking weed. How often do you do that?'

'It was my first time.'

Tom didn't seem to argue. He must have believed me. 'Well, your eyes look pretty bloody red.' We took the turnoff to the main road and headed out of town. 'Bloody drugs. I don't know why you kids think it's so cool.'

'Don't call me a kid,' I blurted.

Tom glanced at me with an amused grin edging the corner of his mouth. 'You have yet to prove to me you're not a kid.'

'So we're picking fruit?' I asked, ignoring his jibe.

'Yeah, maybe …' Tom said. He pushed a CD into the player. Music thumped from the speakers. 'Put your seat belt on.'

I did what he said. I yawned widely. 'I'm hungry.'

Tom laughed. 'There's some apples I picked this afternoon behind the driver's seat. Dig in, munchie girl.'

'What?'

'Nothing.'

I found a large green apple and quickly devoured it. God, I felt hungry. The frothy juice dribbled from my lips. Tom put his forefinger out and rubbed it against my chin, and then pushed it into my mouth. I sucked the acidy juice from his finger, then bit it playfully. I giggled. I couldn't help it. Everything was so funny today. I wound down the window and hurled the apple core outside.

Goodbye little apple—go make lots of apple trees.

Tom's hand was on my leg. He was running it up and down my bare thigh. He curled his hand over to my inner thigh and ran up and down again. I stared ahead, fixated on the white lines of the road that rolled under the car one after the other. His hand hovered at the top of my leg, just below the hem of my school dress, and then glided back down to my knee. I put my hand on top of his.

He looked over and smiled at me. 'Did you like our kiss, Ed?' he asked.

'Like it? I couldn't stop thinking about it,' I said.

'Did you tell anyone?' Tom asked quickly.

'No. You said not to.' So it was a lie. I felt a small twinge of fear. What would he do if he found out I'd told my school friends? He wasn't going to find out from them. I made a mental note to tell Becky to be sure she kept it a secret.

'Good.' He seemed satisfied.

'How much further?'

'The turnoff is just past these pine trees,' Tom said, lifting a finger from the steering wheel and pointing to the left.

There they were: acres of pine trees, piled practically on top of one another, emerald green and so thick it was probably completely dark underneath just metres from the plantation's edge. They seemed to form a massive wall—like some kind of impenetrable fortress. The ground below was carpeted with brown pine needles.

We turned off the main road and headed up the unsealed dirt track to Tom's farm. Barbed-wire fences whirled past me as the car bumped roughly up the road.

'So are you going to kiss me again?' I chanced, turning to smile coyly at him.

'Do you want me to?'

I smirked and ran my hand through my hair. I didn't answer. Of course I wanted him to kiss me.

As the car climbed over the hill I saw an imposing white sandstone house with black windows and a black tiled roof come into view. The garden was neat. There were two massive pine trees in the front garden just near a window. More pines trailed up the edge of the unsealed driveway that ran parallel to the side of the house. The deep-set tyre marks of the driveway were separated by a grass island, and more long green grass carpeted the ground beneath the pines. The land fell away behind the trees and ran down to a wire fence. On the other side the grass was yellow and dry.

'Stay here. Keep your head down,' Tom said, getting out of the car.

'Why?' I said.

'Just stay a minute—okay?'

'Why?'

Tom stared at me for a moment, shook his head, and then turned and walked towards the house.

Crouched down in my seat, I peered over the dashboard at Tom as he went around the house and disappeared from view.

I leaned over into the back seat and pulled out my pencil case from my school bag. I found a pencil and started to play noughts and crosses in the checks on my school skirt. It was so quiet out here—hardly a sound. The sky was reddening. Dusk was coming. I wondered what time it was. It would be dark soon. How were we going to go fruit picking in the dark? My head felt dizzy.

Tom came back to the car. He got in and started the engine, and drove further up the driveway and over the hill.

'What did you have to do?' I said from my slumped position.

'Nothing. It doesn't matter.'

'Oh.' I sat up straighter. 'Where are we going? We don't have long to pick fruit. It's getting dark.'

Tom glanced at me briefly and then looked ahead, neglecting to answer.

I thought his silence was strange. Was I coming across as a silly little girl asking too many questions?

The car puttered quietly over the bumpy uneven ground. Thick yellow grass surrounded us. Pussytail heads bumped against the window as we ploughed through it. I saw an old corrugated iron shed. Rusted farm equipment lay like a graveyard around the side; yellow grass jutted out here and there and even grew right through. An old wagon wheel leaned against the wall, beaten and rusted, the wood rotting and eaten away by termites. A car body lay at the back—I think it was an old ute, the tray completely missing and mounds of grass and thick weeds growing out of it.

Tom stopped the car. 'Stay there a minute.' He got out and went inside the shed. A few seconds later he came back. 'Come on—I want to show you something.'

I swung my legs out and into the long grass. It tickled the insides of my thighs, and crackled under my feet as I followed Tom to the shed. 'What's in there?' I asked as I neared the entrance.

Tom reached over and put his hand on the back of my neck, running his fingers lightly back and forth at the nape. He gave me shivers. 'We shear sheep in here.' A dilapidated wooden door that looked to be hanging by one hinge left a small gap barely wide enough to give entrance to the shed. Tom huddled over, and ducking past the cobwebs that were woven thickly above us, slipped through the gap, firmly gripping my hand. It was practically dark—a few cracks between the wooden planks shed long strips of the bright yellow sunset across the dirt floor, dust visibly rising in the light. Hay bales were stacked in one corner, a few broken apart scattering the dead yellow straw unevenly across the room. Above us, balanced on the decaying wooden rafters, were several large plastic bottles of some green farm chemical and many rusted brown vegetable tins, their faded and discoloured labels peeling away. The shed smelled faintly of animal manure, the dirt floor covered with dried-up animal droppings. It was disgusting. I wondered why he had brought me here.

'What are they?' I asked as I stared up at the menacing iron hooks that hung from the rafters.

'They're for hanging sheep carcasses on.'

'Do you kill them?'

'I do ... sometimes,' Tom said, looking up. 'The sheep make a bloody horrible noise. Their tongues hang out and their eyes roll back in their heads. Even when you stick the knife in and break their necks, their legs don't stop twitching for several minutes afterwards.'

I thought about my mum's lamb chops. I wondered how Tom could do such a cruel thing.

'Come here,' he said.

I stepped closer. He put his hand out and behind my head, cupping it as he pulled me towards him. He leaned down and kissed me. 'I thought we could do this for a while,' he said, coming up for air.

'Okay.' So we were going to make out. He'd brought me here to make out. Well, I guess no one would find us, that was for sure.

'Remember,' he said, tapping his finger lightly on the tip of my nose.

'I know—I can't tell anyone. Anyway, I'm picking fruit right now,' I said flippantly.

'Good girl,' Tom said, clutching my waist and drawing me tightly against him. He kissed me again, his lips delivering more pressure than before. I rested my hands on his shoulders and kissed him back. It was so exciting. I hoped he thought I was a good kisser.

His mouth trailed around to my ear; his tongue glided over my earlobe and then down my neck and under my chin and back up to my mouth. I found myself gasping for air as his mouth left mine and travelled back down towards the V-neck of my dress. With one hand still firmly grasping my waist, his fingertips fumbled with the large blue buttons. My hands trembling, I willingly assisted him. I dared to glance into his eyes as they glowed down on me with his smile that knew, as I did, he was about to touch my breasts. Just as Matty Rogers did to Becky, Tom was about to do to me. I was going to have my first real experience. Finally it was happening to me.

The third button undone, the material lapel of my school dress gaped open and the white lace of my bra was revealed. Breathing heavily, he slipped his hand inside the cotton material and his warm fingers encircled my breast, caressing it gently. His excited eyes searched mine and a pleased, satisfied smile crept over his face. I allowed the heady moment to claim my grip on reality, and with my eyes half closed and lips parted, I awaited another warm, soft kiss.

It wasn't to come. His hand seized my breast with a force so painful, I cried out involuntarily from the shock.

'Hey!' I said, clasping his hand with mine and trying to pull his hand away. He wasn't letting go. 'Hey!' I said again. His breathing was suddenly acutely rapid; his eyes looked transfixed and he didn't appear to hear me. 'Tom!' I cried out again, attempting to wriggle free.

He chuckled a moment and then pressed his forehead against mine with his nose touching my nose. He fixed his blue eyes directly on me and smiled. 'It's okay,' he whispered, gradually releasing my breast, his hand still cupping it. He studied my face a moment and waited for me to say something.

'It hurt a bit, that's all. It's okay now,' I said, smiling weakly, with some relief. I wasn't quite sure what had just happened. He obviously didn't realise how hard he'd squeezed. Maybe he just got carried away. I didn't think for a second that he wouldn't be sorry. Maybe he didn't realise that this was all new to me. I wanted to say that I was nervous but I didn't. What would he think if he knew I hadn't been with a guy before? I didn't want to disappoint him. I didn't want to be my age with him. I wanted to be older. I wanted him to think I could handle it. I wanted to impress him. I guess he probably expected more.

He slipped his hand inside my dress again and his strong fingers closed over my breast. He squeezed it, digging the tips of his fingers into my flesh. 'Tom!' I gasped. God—it really hurt. This time I tried to drag his hand away, gripping his wrist. I wasn't strong enough.

He shook his head. 'Don't you like it? It's supposed to feel good, Edwina. Don't you feel anything?' he whispered into my ear, squeezing my other breast, still with the same painful force. I was confused. Was this really supposed to feel good? I didn't understand. It hurt so much I felt tears welling in my eyes. *That's it, Edwina, cry like a baby. Cry like a baby, Edwina, when things don't go exactly the way you want them to.*

'Oh, come on, Edwina—this is what you want,' Tom said in an annoyed and impatient tone, nuzzling his mouth over my neck, shoving my head back until I gazed up without choice at the meat hooks that dangled above me. 'I know you want me.'

A strange, almost indescribable heat stirred deep inside. It started in the very pit of my being and twisted its way quietly through my stomach, which coiled into tight little knots. My chest felt like it was caving in on me, constricting and suffocating the air that I'd breathed freely moments before. Something that I couldn't quite grasp was not right. Fear wielded an enormous sledgehammer that landed squarely in my chest.

His hand was moving quickly under my skirt, inside my underwear, his cold fingers wandering and invading me. I felt nothing except the sense of his presence. Was I supposed to feel something down there? I couldn't feel anything. What was I supposed to feel?

'It feels good, doesn't it, Edwina?' Tom said, his breathing loud in my ear, his other hand clutching my waist and holding me firmly against him.

I didn't answer. I couldn't answer. My heart was in my mouth. I couldn't speak. No words would come. How did it get this far so fast? I wasn't ready. Was it supposed to happen like this?

He planted his foot firmly on the ground just inside mine, and with the strength of his leg forced my legs further apart. My sandshoes slid on the dirt carpet beneath us. I felt the hardness of his crotch pressing against my thigh. His fingers worked their way inside me, stabbing at me like blunt knives. I bit my bottom lip and tasted blood. I blinked away the tears that clouded my vision. Panic and terror took me over, and I knew I didn't want this. I struggled to pull away from him. His grip strengthened. I choked on the lump that had wedged firmly in the back of my throat. The walls were closing in on me. *Say it, Edwina. Say 'stop' and it will be over. Say it. You can say it. Be brave. He has to stop. He has to stop if you ask. Just say it.*

As if second guessing me, Tom whispered into my ear, his excited breath carrying words that could not be challenged—they were a demand. 'Edwina, get down on the ground.' He said it with such insistence and yet with such composure. 'You want this, Edwina. I know you want it. Get down.'

My knees, already trembling and weak, crumpled beneath the weight of his hands on my shoulders as I obeyed his command. My heart was thumping. My head was struck down with a consuming dizziness that made the room spin before me. I felt ill, nauseated. He was unzipping his jeans. His heavy body pinned me to the ground. One of his strong hands firmly grasped my two wrists somewhere behind my head; the other was between his legs, guiding himself inside me. He was pressing himself relentlessly, relentlessly, until he had completely invaded me. 'Come on, Edwina,' he begged. 'Just let me. You know you want this.'

I wanted to scream, but nothing would come out. I couldn't think straight. I could hardly even breathe. A torrent of unconnected thoughts battled in my head. *Do this. Be a big girl. This is it. It's now. This is happening now. He says you want it. You want this, don't you?*

No, Edwina. Stop him, said another voice. *Get up and run. Run through the paddock. Run into the pine trees and disappear ...*

A dagger drove between my legs. A searing pain seized sharply and my body lurched forward.

Just shut up! the voice answered back. *Shut up and deal with it. Give him what he wants. He's inside you—it's too late. It's just all too late. If you were going to say stop, you can't, you can't stop this, you just can't—*

Scream, Edwina. Scream! Get up. Get up and run. Run—please ... Oh God ... Where will you run? There's nowhere to run. Who will hear your scream? Who will hear it out here, far, far from anywhere?

He thrust harder, rocking back and forth, his hand sliding on my wrists with slippery sweat that rubbed and chafed like sandpaper. Desperate, heavy sobs from deep within me couldn't seem to find their way out. They were trapped, just as I was.

Don't cry. Swallow hard. Don't cry. This isn't happening. Come on. You can make it. Stop, stop, stop ...

The pain gradually began to drift somewhere far, far away. Dying off. Disconnecting. Disconnection came with such sweetness, such relief ... floating from my body up to the shoddy old roof of that shed.

Darting between the gaps in the roof, searching for what

little sunlight remained, and bathing in it momentarily before diving back down, tripping on the wind that quietly whistled through the cracks of the wooden planks; swirling around the rafters faster and faster. Flying, weaving between the old vegetable tins, and circling somewhere high above these two people locked together on the dirty yellow grass bed that was the shed floor.

A man's bare back was creamy white and dotted with freckles. His jeans unbuckled, loosely hanging below his bared backside; the buckle dangling and hitting the ground with a rhythmic jingling. He rocked back and forth over a girl; making small grunting and gasping sounds. Sounds she no longer heard. She heard nothing but silence.

The girl's eyes were fixed somewhere above, her own body motionless beneath him. She didn't blink. Her lips pressed firmly together, she was close to expressionless. She seemed to be part of, but not one with him.

It was too late now. It was too late to change anything. Time could not be taken back. The moment had passed.

A loud cry jolted her and she was again in her body.

Tom pulled away, gasping, and rolled over on his side.

His fingers stroked my cheek. He leaned on one arm and his blue eyes smiled down on me. His hair was wet with sweat and strands of his dark fringe stuck to his forehead. My arms floated from behind my head, released from the heavy weights that had pinned them down. They rested freely over my stomach. The air seemed clearer now. I could breathe. His fingers were cold as they glided over my face. I did not flinch; did not react; did not move.

'That was good, Edwina. I knew it would be good.'

He hoisted himself off the ground and took my hand, helping me up. He helped to straighten up my school dress and smooth out my hair, removing twigs and grass that had caught up in the tangles. He took my hand and guided me out to the car as if I couldn't find my way there alone. The warm wool seat covers stroked my thighs once more.

The car was a capsule of silence as we drove back to town. He didn't put the radio on. He didn't speak to me. His hands travelled the circumference of the leather-covered steering wheel, over and over again. I noticed his fingers were stained, but it wasn't the dark grape juice of the vineyard that normally discoloured his skin. The stains seemed like blood.

Strong hands circled around and around the wheel. I watched their hypnotic action until my head lolled forward and the blackness closed in on me. I have a vague recollection of the car wheels ripping to a halt, and the car door flinging open. Tom was there, holding back my hair. I vomited lumps of warm apple down the side of the car.

'Bloody pot, Ed. You shouldn't be doing drugs at your age, they're bad for you. Have a look at yourself. You hardly know what you're doing. Here,' he said, standing my limp body up, and leaning it like a mannequin against the cold steel of the car. 'You need some fresh air for a minute.'

A car sped past us on the highway at over one hundred clicks. The noise seemed to come from the recess of my mind. The headlights descended into the distance, immersing us back into moonlight. The noise of crickets called to me from the long grass of the nearby paddock, trying in vain to wake me from my daze. Tom leaned into the car and turned the interior light on. He chuckled as he drew himself back out of the car.

'You've bled on the car seat!' He said it almost joyfully—like he was proud of it or something. 'Come on, get in,' he said, his hand on my back, turning me towards the car door.

I climbed robotically into the seat. My stomach felt flat; completely hollow—just as I was. Void. Empty. No longer filled up with him.

In my driveway he handed me a bucket of apricots. 'Here you go. Now remember, we've been fruit picking.' I nodded. He carried several more buckets of fruit that had been stored in the boot of his car into the house.

'Edwina!' Mum shrieked, taking the bucket of apricots from me. 'Look at your school dress!'

Tom's eyes widened and he took a slow step backwards.

Hot prickles rushed through me, awakening the strange numbness that had consumed me on the way home. 'It's just a food stain.' I said quietly.

Mum shook her head at me and then turned to Tom. 'Thank you for the fruit, Tom. It's very kind of you. I hope Edwina was able to help you?'

'She was, Mary. She was a big help.' Tom smiled at me and winked. He excused himself and left.

'What are we going to do about that stain, Edwina? You do have school tomorrow. I can't soak your dress at this time of night and expect it to be ready by morning.'

'I think I can get it out.'

'Hey, Mary! That medical doco is on—do you want to watch it?' my father called loudly from the living room. I heard the TV music in the background.

'Okay, Shaun. I'll be there in a jiffy,' Mum yelled over her shoulder. She turned to me. 'I think if you sponge it with a bit of soap it should come out without too much trouble.'

'Okay.'

Mum paused a moment. 'Are you all right, Edwina? You look—I don't know ...'

'Uh huh.' The words, *I'm fine*, just didn't want to follow.

For a moment she seemed to hesitate, but then she said, 'Hang your dress on a coathanger in the laundry after you sponge it, eh?' And with that she went into the living room.

I went to the bathroom and locked the door. Taking a wash-cloth from the vanity drawer, I soaked it under the tap. I sponged the chocolate ice-cream stain. I noticed the game of noughts and crosses and I scrubbed that away too. I also sponged the dark blood that had dried on the inside of my thighs and on the back of my school dress.

I paused for a moment. I shoved the washcloth back under the tap and turned the hot water on to full. I let it run until the steam clouded the mirror and the water scalded my hands. Grasping the towel rail, I drew the washcloth over the mirror, clearing the condensation. A stranger stared back at me, trapped on the other side. Her green eyes, hollow and defeated, wandered despairingly to the floor and failed to meet mine.

Then, slowly, she turned away. She didn't stop to look back.

CHAPTER 9

At lunch time I sat at the back of the school library drawing on the cover of my portrait pad with a blue biro. Becky had asked to meet me at the canteen, but I lied and told her Mr Habermeil wanted to speak to me about my maths assignment.

I had decorated my art pad at the beginning of the year with photos of friends, and Mum had helped me to laminate it. In the centre was a large photo of Becky and me. Our smiling faces stared out from the cover.

I sat drawing spirals, running the pen around and around the edge of the photo. Gripping the pen, I drove it down hard over my face until the plastic cover ripped. I stabbed it through, dragging it and digging holes. Hot, stinging tears welled in my eyes.

'Are you all right, dear?' a voice asked. I turned to see Mrs Appleton, a library volunteer, stacking books on a shelf behind me. I hadn't realised she was there.

I didn't answer her. I quickly shoved my art pad in my bag, swung it over my shoulder and stormed past her, out of the library.

'Kids today. Honestly!' I heard her mutter.

CHAPTER 10

On Saturday night Mum announced we were going to the Arcoona Creek Dance. God, I hated those stupid dances. Arcoona Creek was in the middle of nowhere, forty minutes' drive outside of Wattleton. Come to think of it, I had never even laid eyes on a creek out there. There was just an old corrugated iron hall in the middle of a paddock with a dirt track leading to the door. While other kids' parents went to the local pub, the football clubrooms, or even the local golf club, *my* parents went to the Arcoona Creek Dance with their church friends. They spent the night whirling around a polished wooden floor to music my Nanna would have listened to when she was like twenty years old—which had to have been over two hundred years ago, I swear. I didn't even understand the names of the pieces of music they played because half of them were in some other language. There was one song they played, though, that we'd learned about in history class called 'It's a Long Way to Tipperary'. It was a wartime song about some girl this guy was desperate to get home and see. They played it at least five times at every dance we went to. My brother George usually sang it on the way home and for half of the next day.

Mum darted around the house frantically just before we left, arranging fairy cakes on a platter and stressing about whether or not to take the whipped cream in a separate container. Dad jigged about, already humming the dance tunes in his head, tapping his foot and clicking his fingers. He was wearing this blue suit thing that had little stretch knit material panels in it. My mum's outfit was a two-piece canary yellow ensemble with frilly bits around her waist. She wore her very best earrings, which sparkled when she shook her head at my father for forgetting to polish his shoes. Matthew and George agonised over which toys they would take with them. Mum said they could take one each because there simply wasn't enough room in the car for everything.

I didn't know what to wear. I chose the plain black dress I'd worn to my cousin's wedding. *Dolly* always says less is more. I figured the black dress was a safe choice because my dad always complained there wasn't much of it.

We stopped and picked up Nanna, who had to sit in the front seat because of her arthritis. That meant my dad had to squash into the back seat with George on his lap, Matthew in the middle, and me alongside. We were driving illegally, and so every time a car drove past us, Mum barked at George to keep his head down, which wound up in Matthew's lap next to him. Matthew tried his best to fart, owing to the close proximity of George's head. George shrieked and Nanna complained that the noise was adding to her migraine—supposedly the same one she'd had for the last twenty years. The car reeked of supermarket perfume and Nanna's hairspray. My dad had tried to tell Nanna some time ago that her hairspray was probably what gave her migraines. She wouldn't have a bar of it. The same as when the doctor tried to tell her that high-heeled shoes were giving her bunions. She'd asked the doctor if he'd got his degree out of a cereal box.

During the car trip to Arcoona Creek, dad mentioned that Tom was coming to the dance. He said he'd invited him many times, and Tom was so sick to death of him pestering him, he'd finally given in. Mum was delighted—that meant one young man she would definitely get a dance with.

With my chin resting on my hand, I stared into the pitch-black nothingness that was the country road. No street lights out here. Nothing but darkness and the glare of white headlights that passed us going in the other direction.

For the millionth time in the past two weeks, I thought about Tom—about his blue eyes, his voice, his raspy breath in my ear.

I closed my eyes and pictured his pale creamy white freckled shoulders. I looked up and saw the meat hooks that dangled from the rafters. I thought about seeing him tonight. My stomach lurched and felt like it would turn me inside out. He would probably avoid me. He would probably see right through me. Now that he had what he wanted, I would be nothing to him. He didn't love me. How could he love me? I was useless. I hadn't gotten anything right. The whole thing the other day—well, that was definitely my fault. It was my fault for not telling him to go slower. It had all happened a bit fast, that was all. It wasn't quite the romantic first time I had hoped for, but so what. There were things I should have said, should have done. But it was over with now. And surely Tom was over me.

Mum had complained that I seemed more self-absorbed than usual. 'You teenage girls, you just get so damned moody. I sure wasn't like that when I was your age,' she said. 'I don't understand you, Edwina. Why won't you talk to me? Why do you have to stay cooped up in your room when you're home? Since when did you stop being part of this family? I'm telling you, Edwina, things are going to have to change. If you think you can get away with this sort of behaviour and still have privileges like meeting your friends after school, you've got another think coming, my girl. I've a good mind to take you to see Reverend Lockhardt and ask him to sort you out. I'm at a loss, Edwina. You can't keep doing this to me. I don't deserve this. I'm your mother, Edwina, and I deserve respect. I have feelings, too. You think life is easy for me? Try running this household for a day and we'll see how you cope. You have no idea how easy you've got it. Life's just one big party of school and friends for you, isn't it? Well, things around here are going to have to change. Starting with your attitude.'

So what if I didn't want to talk to her or anyone else in my family? So what if I wanted to sit in my room? Why did any of them care? They never cared before. They didn't care where I was when I was out with Tom. They didn't ask me what I did out at the farm. They didn't notice it had been dark for over an hour by the time I arrived home. They didn't care. Just like Tom wouldn't care.

When we arrived at the dance hall and piled out of the car, it was bloody freezing. Every breath you let out clouded in front of you like pounds of floating cotton. I stomped my feet up and down just to stay warm. Just inside the entrance to the hall, Mum gave a coin donation to the doorman. He raised his bushy white eyebrows at her as if to say, *Is that all?* She spoke loudly about the fairy cakes and how she had slaved over the oven that afternoon and then promptly headed for the kitchen.

The hall was lined with bracketed wooden chairs. Everyone sat around the edges underneath the colourful assortment of fur jackets that hung from the hooks above. The ladies put their sparkling clutch purses under their seats and held their hands together politely in their laps. The men, in their thin neatly pressed cotton shirts, huddled together outside in the close to zero temperature, smoking cigars and swigging their hip flasks of port.

There was hardly a person in the room under the age of seventy, or at least it seemed that way—just like the Wattleton supermarket on pension day. I'm not sure if that was a blessing or a curse. What I did know was that I was already bored out of my mind. I began to think about supper, with all those lovely pikelets and scones with whipped cream and jam. I didn't know how Anne-Marie did it. Who in their right mind would give up eating?

A tall wrinkly old man with a toupee sprinkled handfuls of sawdust from a cereal box across the length of the dance floor. My brothers saw this as the perfect opportunity to take a running jump and scoot from one end of the hall to the other on the slippery coat-tail of the sawdust. As soon as Mum returned from the kitchen, they scurried back to their seats and played with their action figures.

The piano music started as Margaret Taper's crooked old

fingers flew across the keyboard, her feet dancing about on the pedals beneath her. There were no music sheets in front of her as usual, and she closed her blue make-up-caked eyes and sang loudly with the music.

The men one by one approached the women, and the women graciously stood and curtsied as they took their hands.

Please don't ask me to dance. Please don't ask me.

A frail old man approached me and I smiled at him half-heartedly. He put out his wrinkled hand and I noticed his nails were thick and yellow like Nanna's toenails, and he had sun spots on his skin. I placed a limp hand in his and stood up. He was seriously sweaty. He clutched my waist and held one hand up in the air. His strength for an old man astounded me. At least I probably wouldn't end up resuscitating him. We followed the circle around the hall. I completely had two left feet. I tried to follow the steps of the ladies in front of me but found myself tripping over my own shoes.

'My name is Archibald. What's yours?' the old man asked.

'Ed,' I said.

'What was that?' he yelled, leaning closer. He had long white hairs growing from inside his ear. No wonder he couldn't hear.

'It's Edwina! My name is Edwina!' I yelled.

'Oh,' he said, nodding. He held his arm high and I was to dive under it and come around again back to his side. That's when I noticed the massive wet patch on his shirt under his arm. Oh God! How completely gross. He was wearing some kind of cheap cologne, but it wasn't nearly as powerful as his BO. I wanted to puke.

One of his large hands was in the small of my back. His other gripped one of my hands, holding it in the air. The feel of his hand on my back made me uncomfortable. I didn't want this old man's hands on me—he was making my skin crawl.

'Excuse me,' I said, wriggling from his grasp. 'I have to go to the Ladies'.'

He nodded and looked disappointed. My mum, from the

other side of the dance circle, glared at me as I left the room.

The Ladies' room was tiny—one little toilet behind a creaky wooden door. Someone had tried to pretty it up with one of those crocheted dolls that cover the toilet roll. Enormous moths flew around the light bulb overhead. I sat down and counted backwards from one hundred.

When I came back to the hall, Tom had arrived. He stood just inside the door paying his entry fee. He was wearing a brown shirt with a navy jumper over the top and jeans with brown RM Williams boots. He looked nice. He looked respectable. His hair was combed back like he'd just washed it.

'Hi, Edwina,' he said when he saw me.

'Hi.'

I watched as he glided up to my mum and planted a kiss on her cheek. He whispered something in her ear. She looked at me, and back at him, and nodded, smiling.

He came over and took my hand. 'Come on, Ed,' he said, 'I'm rescuing you.' And with that he was dragging me out the door. I looked over my shoulder at my mum, who smiled, waving the back of her hand as he ushered me out. I stepped out into the cold darkness.

'Where are we going?' I asked.

'I'm getting you out of that retirement village for a while. Get in the car,' he said, opening the door. I didn't get in. I stood there looking at him. For a moment he stared at me and then, looking back to the hall, he put his hand up to my cheek. 'Look, Ed,' he said in a quiet voice, 'we didn't get a lot of time together the other day. I want to know about you—is that so bad? You're so sweet, Ed.' He was stroking my hair, tucking it behind my ear. 'You're special to me, Ed. I want us to get to know each other some more.' He tapped my nose. 'Come on, we're wasting time standing here. Get in the car.'

I didn't say anything, but I got in and put my seatbelt on. So he still liked me—amazing. He wasn't angry at me. He jumped in the driver's seat.

'What did you say to my mum?' I asked.

'There's a present back there on the seat, see.' I turned around to see a carefully wrapped present in beautiful pink tissue paper with a huge wide blue ribbon. I wondered momentarily if it was for me.

'It's for Mrs Appleton, from my mother,' he explained. 'I told your mother I needed you to wrap it for me—that I'd only just collected it from lay-by from the chemist gift shop.'

'But it's already wrapped.'

'Yeah,' he said, smiling at me. He started the engine and turned out through the barbed-wire gate and drove further up the track.

'Where are we going?' I asked.

'Not far.'

He was right. No sooner had we taken off than we had stopped again. He turned off the engine and the headlights. There was condensation on the car windows. The car had not driven long enough to warm up. Outside I could see the vague outline of what I thought was a tree or a very large shrub. I thought it was someone watching me. *What are you doing, Edwina? What are you doing in there?*

Tom leaned over and pushed his cold hand up under my dress until it rested between my legs. I held my breath.

'Ed,' he said quietly, 'I think you're beautiful.'

The word seemed to bounce right off me. *Me? Beautiful?* Not in the same sentence! No one had ever called me beautiful before. No one. It sounded so nice. He sounded like he meant it. I reached up and touched his face and waited. Waited to hear that word again, and perhaps the words of love that might follow.

With his left arm, he reached behind me and was fumbling around for something. I felt the seat tip back. 'We have to be quick, Ed,' he said, climbing over on top of me. 'They'll be waiting for us.' He was pushing my dress up until it bunched around my waist. He started to undo his belt buckle.

I heard my words almost as if someone else had spoken

them. 'I'm not ... I don't really want—'

'Shh, Ed. It'll be good. You'll see.'

'No. I really don't ... My parents ... They ...'

He cut me off. 'Christ!' He let out a long sigh, supporting himself above me on the strength of one arm, the other running through his thick hair and then landing with a loud frustrated thud on the car door. I froze with fright. He glared at me for a moment and then he pulled back. I felt relief. It wasn't going to happen. He wasn't going to take it any further. That had been all I needed to say last time and he would have stopped. It was my fault—last time—because I hadn't spoken. It had definitely been my fault.

Without any warning, the seat slid back. He was wriggling himself backwards until he crouched in the small space below the glove compartment. His strong hands on my thighs, he pushed my legs apart. I tried to sit up, but he put out his arm and pushed me back down.

'I'm going to show you something, Ed,' he said in a firm voice. 'Just lie there. Lie still. Don't move. You'll like it, I promise.'

It felt wrong, very, very wrong—him down there and me with my legs apart lying on the seat. But he was so insistent. Insistent that it would all be fine if I just let him do it. I felt him pushing my legs with his elbows, one hand pressing firmly on my stomach, the other one between my legs. He pulled my underpants to one side. I felt the warmth of his breath as he came closer. Panic seized my chest. It was as if someone was thumping me in the stomach, winding me until I could hardly breathe. Oh God, what was he going to do?

'No, no ...'

'Aw, c'mon, Ed,' he said, like a parent to a child. 'Listen to me. You want to go out with me—be my girlfriend? I thought you were more grownup than this. That's why I like you, Ed. You're not like the other girls your age.' He stroked my leg with his hand and kissed it softly. His lips glided over my thigh and travelled upwards until I felt the warmth of his breath again.

My reaction was automatic—I wriggled myself back from him, but I didn't have anywhere to go. His strong hands clutched my hips, drawing me to him.

'Tom, I—'

'Just shush up, Ed. It's okay. I'm just going to kiss you. It's just kissing—kissing can't be wrong, can it?'

I guess it couldn't.

The dark figures outside the window watched me. Scowled at me. Judged me. They swayed silently outside like dark evil beings—watching me, watching him.

'Does it feel good, Ed? You're so soft,' he said breathlessly, his tongue leaving me and kissing the inside of my thigh.

His muffled voice came from miles away—out of the depths of the darkness. Feel? I didn't know what I was supposed to feel. There was nothing. I could only feel his mouth. I couldn't feel me. I was totally numb. I didn't know how to respond. I didn't know what to say. I didn't even know people did this. I was convinced that it was happening to me, only to me, and no one else in the world knew of this terrible act—this thing he was doing with his mouth.

'Come on, Ed. You're supposed to feel something. Don't you feel anything?' He sounded frustrated. Why wasn't I performing for him? Why wasn't I reacting like I should? His frustration ate at me. It formed words in my mind. *You're useless, Edwina, useless. You stupid little girl. Can't you get it right?*

The condensation dripped down the window and formed little droplets of dew. I watched their trail, one meeting with another and forming a larger droplet. They were like little stars against a black night sky.

The black figures loomed outside the window; they surrounded the car, compressing the confined space tightly around me. The wool of the seat covers was the only gentleness I felt. Tom's hair brushed my stomach, his head moving quickly as his mouth worked roughly back and forward.

Bring the end. Make it stop. How long does this need to go on for?

Please bring the end.

'Don't you feel it, Ed? Doesn't it feel good?'

My nails dug into the seat, clenching it tightly. No other part of my body moved. I was rigid with fear. Fear of what he was doing. Fear I couldn't get it right. Fear he would hate me because I didn't understand.

'Don't you feel *anything*?' he demanded in an irritated voice.

I could tell he wanted me to say yes, I just didn't know what to say to make him believe me. Maybe if I said yes, it would stop?

'Yes, I think so. I'm not sure ...'

I heard him sigh. He was clearly disappointed in my reaction. I had failed him again.

He suddenly pulled himself up and, with an agitated grunt, climbed back over into the driver's seat. 'Pull your skirt down,' he said angrily. I did as he said. He set the seat back to the upright position. He clutched the steering wheel and stared through the windshield at nothing.

'Let's go.' He started the engine and drove back to the hall. His silence spoke a million words. I had failed him. I was useless and I had failed him. When he parked the car, he gazed at the hall and then turned to me. His voice changed. He smiled and his hand ran through my hair. 'I'll arrange to pick you up tomorrow, Ed. Your mother will let you come to my farm fruit-picking again.' His voice was suddenly calmer. He spoke almost quietly.

Free fruit for my mum? Of course she would. 'Yes,' I answered.

'Good.'

He climbed out, came around to my side and opened the door. 'The Pride of Erin' blared from the dance hall. He held my arm firmly, just below my shoulder.

'I think I'm falling in love with you, Ed.' He smiled, his blue eyes looking directly at mine. 'I can show you things, Ed. I can love you, if you let me. You have to let me, though. Just try to relax, eh? I'm not going to hurt you. I haven't hurt you, have I? What we just did ... Well, it just feels weird the first few times.

You'll start to like it soon, I promise you. People who love each other do that.'

Looking over at the hall, he placed his large hands either side of my face. My head was like a walnut in a vice. He leaned down and kissed me. 'And ... I think I love you,' he whispered.

Love me? The useless little girl who can't get it right?

We headed back into the hall, but only after Tom passed me the present—the reason I had gone with him in the first place.

Maybe this was how love was. It wasn't quite as I had imagined it.

CHAPTER 11

At Tom's farm in the middle of the grassy paddock was a little blue tent. It seemed odd, out here in the middle of nowhere. Inside there were sleeping bags, a CD player and packets of lollies.

'Why do you have this here?' I asked. The tent wasn't tall enough for me to comfortably stand, so I knelt down on the softness of the sleeping bags, feeling the hard uneven earth beneath.

'I slept out here last night,' he answered. I couldn't imagine why—why he had slept out here away from his house and his own bed. As if reading my mind he added, 'I needed to get away from everything, you know?' I knew what that meant, I guess.

He lay back on the sleeping bag and unzipped his jeans. In bright daylight—there it was. The ugliest damned thing I have ever seen. I knew what it was, but something in my head wasn't quite connecting with the fact it was *his*. Like it was a photograph I was looking at—like this wasn't for real. Like this tiny little blue tent and everything in it was completely removed from the real world.

'I want you to ...' He put his finger in my mouth.

I didn't understand what I was supposed to do. Surely he didn't mean ... I knelt motionless next to him.

Putting his hand behind my neck, with limited force he brought my head down until it hovered just above his unzipped jeans. 'Just like one of those lollipops I've seen you eat, you know, just like that.'

The side of the tent was centimetres from me. The fine plastic fibres were basket-woven. It's amazing the detail you can see in things—things you would never have noticed unless you took the time to look. I focused on the side of the blue tent, noting the stains, differentiating between the thickness of the material where the light from outside dissolved through and where it didn't. The fine line of machine stitching that held the panels together.

There were no words. There was the silence of an empty paddock bar the shrill whistle of the wind that drew the walls in and out, flapping the unzipped entrance. I waited for someone to burst through the opening and see me. *Edwina, what are you doing?* He kept a firm hand on my head, holding me there. I struggled to breathe, finally breathing out through my nose instead. He shoved my head up and down roughly, gripping my hair like it was the reins. My eyes watered, trickling small lines down my cheeks. I was gagging. Pulling back with what little room he gave me to, I made him hit the roof of my mouth.

I don't remember leaving the tent. I don't remember much except the vivid blue walls that surrounded me. Time was not part of this world. Time meant nothing out here, out here with Tom. Time lingered on and on and yet stood still. Time only started again when Tom gave the order.

We neared the edge of the pine tree plantation. He parked his car and we got out. He took my hand and led me to the edge, through the gap in the fencing, and over to a tree where he pushed me back against the rugged bark and kissed me.

'Let's play a game, Ed,' he whispered.

A game? I wondered what kind of game he had in mind.

'I want you to run, Ed. Run into the trees. I'll count, and then I'm going to chase you. And when I catch you, Ed, I get to kiss you. Are you ready?'

I nodded.

'One ... two ... three ...'

I ran.

'Don't look back, Ed!' he called.

I ran, darting in and out of the trees. There was no clear space to run—the trees were intermittent in their placement—over hilly mounds of dead pine needles; dodging the dappled grey and chocolate-coloured tree trunks, running deeper into the darkness of the pines. The sky closed in, dissolving the blue and the little sunlight that broke through. The quiet eerie crackle of the forest surrounded me. I ran and ran, hearing only the pounding of my feet and the rapid rasp of my breath. *Run hard, Edwina ... Be good at this game ...*

Eventually I staggered to a breathless standstill. I could see nothing but the trunks of pine trees in either direction. Where was he? I searched for a hint of movement, the material of his shirt. But there was nothing. Was I going crazy? He was right behind me, wasn't he? He was chasing me, right?

I leaned against a tree and breathed the deep sweet scent of the pines. Where was he? I gazed around and realised just how alone I was all of a sudden, how far I was from anyone. Which way was the edge—which way was out? I called out his name. There was no answer. A growing fear sat in the back of my mind, waiting for me to take its hand and lead it out here with me, out into the loneliness of the forest.

I started walking. I hoped I was going in the right direction. I had taken so many twists and turns. Where was he? Had I hidden myself that well? Why couldn't he hear me calling him? The ground was uneven. I began to imagine the little mounds were where bodies lay, buried beneath the brown pine needles among the darkness like a long forgotten graveyard. I waited for a hand to strike out, reaching from the blanket of needles, and clutch at my ankles.

It grew lighter; I had found the plantation's edge. I couldn't see Tom. I looked for his car. It was gone. This was where he had parked, wasn't it? Surely I hadn't gone that far? Where was he? Surely he wouldn't leave me here?

Disoriented, I sat down next to a tree, close enough to be concealed, but with a view of anyone approaching. Perhaps I should still be playing the game? It was hide-and-seek. Would he be angry with me for not hiding properly?

I listened to the lonely whisper of the forest. The sobs I heard were mine, though I don't know that I really registered them. Confusion clouded my head.

I heard a car engine. It was Tom. I gasped with relief to see him. Relief I was no longer alone. 'Where did you go?' I said, standing up.

'I had to do something,' he replied, taking my hand and leading me back into the forest.

My mind and my heart led me also. I was on a romantic walk. He was holding my hand. It was a beautiful forest full of nature's beauty. We were lovers, locked hand in hand on a perfect day.

He took off his jumper and laid it on the ground like a picnic rug. He told me to sit on it—on the big red and black chequered picnic rug. Soon he would pour champagne from a wicker basket and present me with a rose or maybe little love-heart-shaped chocolates. He would whisper he loved me and lean in and kiss my cheek. A squirrel would scamper around us and pick at the basket searching for bread rolls. We'd both throw our heads backward and laugh, lost in some kind of stupid Disney movie.

Parts of the blue sky hung above—no clouds, but pure light blue sky. The tree tops swayed, sometimes almost touching one another. Soon I was there, up in the trees. High, high above the two people on the ground. There was that girl's face again. She was motionless, like a rag doll—her blank eyes stared into an empty vacuum. Isolated in the forest, she lay partially naked beneath a man with the pine needles biting at her stiff doll-like legs. Her lips slightly parted, she didn't appear to be breathing. Her face was colourless.

She awoke to the man's voice—the only thing that brought her in and out of consciousness like some kind of mysterious commander of her soul.

'I said, are you all right?'

'Why?' she said.

'You were staring. You were staring and not answering me.'

He looked concerned, maybe even a little frightened.

She placed a weak hand on his chest, motioning for him to release her. He surveyed her face for a minute; appeared satisfied she was indeed all right, and then continued to thrust himself inside her.

The pine trees held me above the girl like angels, their branches like wings, cupping me and holding me high in the air, in the safety of their place in the world. It didn't matter what he did to that girl down there. It didn't matter what she wanted. He was running this game. She was a participant: willing or unwilling was of no relevance to him.

He held my hand, leading me out of the forest and into the glare of daylight. I walked beside him, clutching his hand, righting myself as I stumbled unsteadily. When I tripped, he pulled me back and, standing behind me, held me still for a moment with his hands on my hips.

I felt his warm breath near my ear. 'See, I take good care of you, don't I?' he whispered. Not waiting for an answer, he slapped me hard on my backside and then headed for his car, leaving me standing there.

'Hurry up, I've got work to get on with,' he called without turning to look back at me.

CHAPTER 12

Mum served us apricots and ice-cream for dessert. My brother George was elated and shovelled large spoonfuls quicker than he could swallow, his small cheeks filling like tight balloons. Matthew ate the ice-cream and strategically avoided the apricots. Dad hummed along with the farm fertiliser ad on TV.

Mum's eyes narrowed at me as I poked the apricots with my spoon. 'So what do you and Tom talk about? You know, when you're fruit picking?' she asked. Her question jarred me. Dad launched into a private rendition of the Motor Mate jingle, tapping his feet under the table. George giggled at him, ice-cream dribbling down his chin. Matthew sucked a lump of ice-cream, spat it back on to his spoon, and then sucked it in again.

'Nothing.'

'Well, surely you talk about something, Edwina?' she asked, eating a small spoonful of ice-cream. I felt like saying, *Why are you interested? What does it matter? Why do you suddenly want to know so much about what's going on in my life?*

'Not much. We just pick fruit.' I scooped a mouthful of apricot. It sat in my mouth. I couldn't swallow it.

'Well, you must talk about something.' She held the spoon close to her mouth; it hovered there as she waited for a response.

'Um ... well, we just pick fruit and he teaches me farming stuff. He's not there the whole time—he goes off and fixes equipment while I pick the fruit,' I lied. I could say anything I wanted and she would believe me, because she believed in Tom—she trusted him. And so did my dad.

She looked at me for a moment longer and seemed to accept I would say no more. I began to gag on the apricot. I got up and ran for the toilet.

Slamming the door behind me, I spat the warm lump of apricot into the bowl. I watched it bob up and down for a minute in the clear water, then I crouched on the floor and shoved my two fingers down my throat until my eyes watered. I vomited until I was gasping for air. I bunched up a lump of toilet paper and wiped my chin.

I sat back against the cold wall and felt calmer. Empty. Cleansed. I thought of Anne-Marie. Perhaps this is why she did this? Because you could do it to yourself and be in total control. Because it was a secret. Because her stomach felt empty, just like mine, and her senses felt strangely alive.

Dad knocked gently on the door. 'Are you all right?'

I put my foot out, holding the door with my sneaker. 'Yeah—I just choked on a piece of apricot. It got stuck in my throat.'

'Can George finish your ice-cream?'

'Sure. I'll be out in a minute.'

I heard him move away. I heard George squeal with delight.

In the bathroom I cleaned my teeth because I still had the taste of vomit on my tongue. I scrubbed away furiously, bumping the roof of my mouth with the head of the toothbrush. It felt strangely sore. I opened my mouth and stared at the mirror. I blinked and staggered sideways for a moment and then, regaining my composure, turned on the mirror light to see better. I tipped my head back as far as I could and opened my mouth wide. I didn't recognise what I was seeing. A blood-red, nearly black blister practically covered the roof of my mouth. I stuck my forefinger in and touched it. It was sore, like a bruise. How did that get there? I stared at my reflection. That girl behind the glass with the vacant eyes stared back at me. Did I do that to myself when I vomited? Surely I didn't cause that, did I? Frightened, I decided never to vomit again, no matter how good it made me feel. And not once did I think of that bruise again—nor the truth about how it *really* got there.

CHAPTER 13

'I can't see you any more,' Tom said, his head rested on the pillow of my bed as he stared up at the ceiling. He lay there, one boot balanced on top of the other, and waved his feet from side to side. I didn't answer him.

I sat on my desk chair watching him crack his knuckles one by one. My family was out. I was supposed to have walked to Nanna's house over half an hour ago. Tom knew that. He knew everything we did thanks to my unwitting father.

'You're too young, Edwina. I'm so much older than you. People are going to talk, you know—if they find out.'

I panicked for a moment that he thought I had said something. That he would be angry. 'I haven't told anyone,' I said quietly.

'Well, you can't. Don't you ever tell anyone. Do you understand?' he said firmly, sitting up and swinging his legs over the side of the bed. He looked strangely out of place all of a sudden. This older man sitting on my pink frilly single bed. A little girl's bed. He clutched a stuffed toy and twisted its head, one way and then another.

'Did I do something?' I asked shakily. *You're so useless, Edwina. You've failed him. You can't get this right.*

He sat silently, just looking at me. Finally he said, 'Nothing, Ed. You're just too young. You can have other boyfriends. Maybe when you're older, maybe we can ...' His voice drifted off.

A single tear dripped down my cheek, running on to my nose and then hanging on the tip. I searched for the tissue box.

He passed it to me. 'The boys talk about you, Edwina. You know, in the footy change rooms. Boys your age like you.'

No they don't, I thought.

He unzipped his jeans and put out his hand. A myriad of unconnected reasons placed my hand mechanically in his. He drew me close to him like a servant to a master. His blue eyes were glassy and blank, devoid of emotion. He got me to kneel down at the side of the bed. 'It's over,' he said, forcing my head down to his crotch.

It went on until my jaw ached, until my whole face was sore and contorted. While the tears ran down my face and I choked for every breath. While he dug his fingers into my tangled hair and yanked my head back and forth, barking orders at me to do it this way, do it that way. Until the heavy, thick, ornately woven lace curtains that hung by my bed became embedded in my memory like a sheet that hung all the way from heaven, delivered down to distract me from the degradation that was killing me off inside.

This was the last time. He had said it was over. I didn't float from my body this time. I didn't glide away to the ceiling. I didn't separate myself from my reality. I lived every second of it until finally, with the strength of one hand, he dragged my head away and cast me off. He stood up and zipped up his jeans. Without looking back, he walked out of my room and slammed the door shut.

That was his way of saying goodbye.

CHAPTER 14

When Matty Rogers stuck his tongue in my mouth as we stood behind the local scouts' hall one Sunday afternoon, I didn't feel anything. Without a single sensation flowing in my body, I kissed him robotically—the same lips that had kissed Tom now kissing Matty. As he clumsily clutched at my chest, it could have been someone else's body he was touching. It didn't occur to him to consider how I felt, whether or not I was enjoying it. That didn't seem to matter to any guy.

Matty wouldn't acknowledge my existence at school. In fact, he actually went out of his way to avoid me. In the company of his mates, he'd allow them to tease me and he'd laugh appreciatively when the other boys made suggestive comments, rolling their eyes and rubbing their hands over themselves, groaning in mock pleasure.

At night, when I climbed into bed, Tom was there with me. He crawled into my head, weaving his way through my exhausted mind making me recall every moment I had been with him. He whispered that if I had done this, done that ... If I'd been better, more attractive, smarter, older ... He wouldn't let me forget he owned me, he owned my body; he owned who I was.

When I woke in the morning he was there, another day he was inevitably part of. When I ate breakfast he told me I was fat and shouldn't have that extra slice of toast. When I got ready for school, he stared back at me from the mirror and told me I would never be pretty; that I would never compare; never be able to compete with the Kylie Baxters of the world. At school, he hammered me when I missed a question on a test, telling me I was stupid and I shouldn't even bother. When I opened my mouth to speak to my classmates, he whispered in my ear, telling me no one believed what I was saying, nobody cared or wanted to hear it. When I walked home from school alone, he told me I would never be a success at anything; that I was destined for Wattleton mediocrity. There was nothing special about me. The dreams I had to travel the world and study art were just that—dreams. I wasn't somehow special, and I wasn't somehow different from anyone else in this little backwater. I wasn't worth jack. Sometimes he even told me I would be better off dead. Sometimes I believed him.

But then a small part of me wouldn't let me go, wouldn't let me give up. I somehow found the strength to go on, seemingly unchanged to those who loved me and were part of my life. I became quite the actress. For some time I'd fool even myself—believing that I could get by. Life would be literally about getting by. It wouldn't be about living. Life would effectively be on hold until I could learn to return the gaze of the girl in the mirror and confront the truth of what Tom had really done to me. To me. Not some other girl. Not the girl I had watched from afar. Not the girl in the mirror. Me.

CHAPTER 15

Becky asked me to stay over at her house. We were going to go to the footy club, though my mum thought I was just sleeping at Becky's. Her parents were cool: they didn't mind us going to the football club together. Becky's dad even let Becky smoke in his company now. I told Mum this one day during an argument. She, predictably, had a fit. She said it was because Becky's dad was so worn out from dealing with Anne-Marie's eating problems that he probably didn't care any more. She told me that other people's kids weren't as loved as I was and that was why she didn't let me do stuff like that. She also said if I dared even put a cigarette to my lips I could kiss goodbye to sleeping at Becky's house ever again.

It had been five months since Tom told me it was over between us. Five whole months. Once I walked down to the tennis courts and peered through the mesh fencing and watched Tom play mixed doubles. I didn't like the girl he was playing with. She had huge breasts that bounced around the court more than the tennis ball did. He made it his aim to grope her every time they won a point. During a break, after he had finally spotted me, he walked right up to the fence and told me to get the hell out of there before someone saw me. No hello. No nothing. How does someone go from sharing the most intimate moments—from being inside you—to not even acknowledging you exist?

I couldn't believe I had managed to keep our relationship secret. There was always someone who knew, wasn't there? Was my dad's favourite grapevine grinding to a halt? It was lucky he hadn't bought shares in it.

I'd turned fifteen. I wasn't allowed to have a party. We couldn't afford one, anyway. I got my denim miniskirt from Sportsgirl, though—the one I had picked out of the catalogue. Mum received it by mail order. It almost didn't make it by my birthday, she said, and that I wouldn't believe the trouble it took to get it to Wattleton. She said she hoped I was grateful and that I didn't deserve it because I had behaved so poorly of late. For once I agreed with her. I told her she was right—that I didn't deserve it. Then she yelled at me more for being a smartarse and for trying to challenge her authority, or some other crap. I stood there and took all of it in, almost enjoying it. She told me to pull my head in before she sent the skirt back.

When I got there, Becky ushered me quickly into her bedroom, where she proudly produced a large bottle of vodka from under her bed. She said that Mardie and Hayley would be joining us soon. She put music on and opened the bottle. We sat down cross-legged on the floor.

'Becky, are you crazy? What if your parents come in?'

'They won't. They respect my privacy,' she said. What a foreign concept that was to me. She poured vodka into a shot glass.

'Bottoms up!' she said, throwing her head back and sinking the vodka. I did the same. It burned the back of my throat.

'Jesus, Becky, can't we mix it with something?' I said, holding my throat.

'Yeah, I've got a bottle of OJ under here, too,' she said, reaching under her bed and fumbling around for it, 'and some plastic cups, I think.'

We heard the doorbell ring and Becky's mum call out, 'Becky, I think it's your friends!'

'Hey, Ed, can you get it? I'm going to pour some drinks.'

I got up and went out to the front door. That's when I noticed Anne-Marie sitting in a recliner chair in the living room. Her glassy stare didn't move from the television when I said hello. I let Mardie and Hayley inside.

'Hi, Ed! Had any healthy carrots lately?' Mardie bellowed, bursting inside with her overnight pack swung over her shoulder.

'Hi.' Her comment irked me. 'Hi, Hales.'

'Hi, Ed.'

I noticed Hayley was wearing a tight fitting T-shirt. Two tiny mounds bobbed proudly from her chest. In my mind, shares in bra manufacturing rocketed ten per cent.

In Becky's room we sat around in a small circle and downed the vodka. Every time Becky poured a glass she hid the bottle back under her bed. That way it looked like we were just drinking orange juice, she said. She passed around the cigarette packet. Mardie announced that she had a small bag of weed just for tonight and we could stop and smoke it on the way to the football club.

'Oh God! I love this song!' Becky shouted, leaping up and turning up the volume. She danced around the room twirling her short skirt and wiggling her bum. Her dark locks fell messily over her shoulders, her large hoop earrings getting tangled in her hair.

I wondered for a moment how this girl dancing could have so much energy, and yet just beyond her bedroom door sat Anne-Marie, wasting herself into oblivion.

'Come on, Ed! Drink up! It's party night. I heard that Brody Hillbank's got the hots for you. Tonight might be your lucky night!' She twirled around the room. Mardie and Hayley lay back on the carpet and laughed at her. 'You're a legend, Becky Cooper!' Mardie yelled. 'An absolute legend!'

Through all the excitement, I couldn't believe Becky's parents let her do this—smoke in her room and have friends over—and didn't complain about the music. Mine would have belted the door down by now.

We pasted on our make-up, painted one another's toenails and styled one another's hair into the perfect look. I privately thanked God I had my new skirt, that for one night I could look like the other girls. My mum was finally letting me shave my legs. She said that waxing was the modern-day equivalent of medieval torture and shaving was less painful, even though you have to do it every day. Surely beauty therapists have to inject you with painkillers before they wax?

We stumbled the whole way to the football club. I was seriously plastered. I thought of Tom and the day he had picked me up, stoned. I wondered if he would be there. Stuff him. I hoped he saw me with another guy.

A sign on the door to the clubrooms said *No ID, No Alcohol*. The doorman eyed us suspiciously as we paid our entry fee. They weren't going to be choosy, though, about who they let in. Not in Wattleton. Not where the population barely paid for a footy club dance.

The room was dark, and a lone disco ball and a few coloured lights sparkled brightly above us. I searched the room for Tom, but I couldn't see him.

'Hey, Eddie, can you hold my jacket?' Becky said. 'I'm busting to pee.'

'Me too,' Mardie said, piling her jacket on top of Becky's.

'Me three!' added Hayley, throwing hers on as well.

I stood next the wall, coats in hand, feeling like an idiot.

'What are you?' Joey Parsons said, leaning into me, schooner glass of Coke in hand, 'a bloody coat rack?'

Joey was in the grade above me. He was good-looking, intelligent in his studies and equally good at sport. He was a full forward in the Colts footy team and the premiership best-on-ground player for the last two years running. He was also the rising star in the Wattleton Cricket Club. I couldn't believe he was talking to me. He moved only in the right circles and I wasn't in the right circle, let me tell you. The right circle in Wattleton was filled with people exactly like Kylie Baxter—cashed-up, good-looking and super-confident. Joey was exactly the kind of guy my mum hoped I would end up marrying and popping out babies with. Mum didn't realise boys like Joey don't pay attention to girls like me.

'Well?' Joey's eyes were totally bloodshot as he stared at me waiting for a response. He was probably as drunk as I was. I knew that it wasn't straight Coke in his glass.

'Rack off, Joey!' I yelled back, above the music.

'Put those rags down and come and dance with me,' Joey said drunkenly, putting one hand on the wall and leaning over me. He swigged his drink. Did he have the wrong person? Why was he talking to me?

'You don't want to dance with me,' I said. 'Find someone else, Joey.'

'Ooh—hold your fire, ma'am!' Joey said, putting both his hands up as if surrendering, clutching his schooner glass between his forefinger and thumb.

I couldn't help but smile. Joey actually seemed to be trying it on.

Suddenly the glass slipped from his fingers and smashed on the parquetry floor beneath us. Coke splashed up and hit my legs. Brody Hillbank came from nowhere and slapped his mate on the back.

'Nice one, Romeo!' Then he turned to me. 'Hi, Ed. You look hot tonight.'

I didn't know what to say. I smiled and looked at my shoes.

The girls returned from the bathroom. Hayley had apparently vomited and Becky had to hold her hair out of the toilet bowl. Becky led her to a chair where she slumped over the table and looked like she'd gone to sleep.

'Smoke?' Joey said, passing me his packet of cigarettes.

'Na,' I said coyly, pushing them back at him.

'Good girl, eh? I like good girls.'

'Hey, Ed,' Brody said smiling widely at me, 'Joey my man here has a new car—wanna take a spin later?'

'Can you drive?' I asked, but too drunk to care whether he could or not.

'Yeah. I haven't had as many as Joey and besides, the copper's in bed now—it's after midnight.'

'Okay.' I wasn't passing up the opportunity to go driving with two of the coolest boys in school. I couldn't believe they were asking me!

'Wanna go now?'

'Now?' I said, looking at the other girls. Becky was smiling. She nodded. 'Okay, what about the other girls? Can they come too?'

'Oh, you can leave the girls here for a bit. Besides, Hayley's already seen Joey's car,' Brody said, laughing. I wondered when Hayley had seen it. 'I don't think she's going anywhere for a while,' he said, looking over at Hayley. We watched as a barman cleared glasses and bottles from her table. He paused to poke her with the bottom of a schooner glass. She lifted an arm at him, as if to signal she was still alive, and then flopped it back down on the table.

'Okay, let's go.'

We left the clubrooms, the music thumping behind us, and headed for the car park. Joey lit another cigarette. His so-called new car was about twenty years old. The body paintwork was cracking and it had dozens of dents and scratches. It was what Dad would have referred to as a 'shit heap'.

Brody and Joey both got into the front bench seat, with Brody at the wheel, and told me to get in the back. Brody reversed out of the car park and wound down the driver's side window. He dangled his cigarette over the ledge.

'Where are we going?'

'Around,' Brody said. We drove through the wrought iron gates of the football club and headed towards the centre of Wattleton. 'Let's do a mainy.'

The song 'Khe Sahn' blared from the speakers. It was like Wattleton's national anthem or something. Everybody loved that song. Everybody knew the words. It didn't matter it was an old song. It was still cool.

We did a mainy and then headed out of town on the road that led to Tom's house. More or less as soon as we took the turnoff, Joey hoisted himself up and climbed into the back seat with me.

'Go for it, mate,' Brody laughed, turning up the stereo. Joey put his arm around me and shoved his hand under my top.

'Joey! Stop that!' I said, pushing him away. But instead he just lunged on top of me and started kissing me. I struggled with him. He reeked of bourbon. 'Joey! Get off of me!' I said, shoving him with all the force I had. 'Get off!'

He clumsily leaned back for a minute and, removing his jacket, swung it on to the front seat. Then he lunged forward again.

Something inside me snapped. This time, when he leaned in to kiss me, I thrust my hand in his face and pushed him until the back of his head hit the car door. He slumped against it and passed out.

I turned to Brody. I don't think I knew at that point I was screaming. I think I was hysterical. 'Turn the car around, Brody! Turn the car around *now,* Brody!'

Brody kept driving.

'Brody, can you hear me? Turn this car around! Take me back to town now!' I shouted at him, every part of me shaking. He didn't respond.

That was it. I was so furious, I grabbed his hair from behind, yanking his head backwards so I could scream in his ear. 'Turn this car around now, Brody Hillbank! Right this second—I mean it.' The car swerved.

'All right!' Brody shouted. 'Jesus!' he cursed, rubbing his ear. He swung the car into a sharp U-turn. I think he almost lost it. I heard the gravel under the tyres, ripping out behind us. I held on to his hair like it was my insurance. When we entered the lower speed zone, I yelled at him again. 'Stop the car! Stop it now!'

He hit the brakes, grinding to an abrupt halt. I flung open the door and ran. I turned back to see Joey's legs hanging out. I saw Brody slam the door and start chasing me. Chasing down my sanity. I was no match for him. He caught me within seconds.

'Let me go, Brody!'

'No!'

'Let me go! Please!'

'No, Ed, just calm down for a minute. We didn't want to hurt you. We were just having a bit of fun.'

'Stop it. Just let me go.' It was useless to fight. I was sobbing uncontrollably. 'Let me go, please. This is what Tom did ... This is what Tom did ... Let me go ...' I don't think I even knew what I was saying.

'I know.'

'What? What do you mean, you know?'

'I know, Ed. All we wanted was for you to give us a little bit too. Please let me be with you, Ed ...'

His words weren't sinking in. They weren't ringing true in my head. What did he mean?

'Oh God, please let me go.'

'Promise, Ed. Promise you'll be with me too one day. Promise me, Ed ...'

'Whatever! Okay! All right! Anything you want! Just let me go!'

He released me. I ran sobbing up the street. I ran and ran, forgetting I was supposed to be sleeping at Becky's house. I ran home and squeezed myself through the side gate, into the car port. I huddled in the corner near the cold weatherboard wall and cried myself to sleep.

The first thing I knew when I woke was that my head felt like it was going to split in two. Everything whirled. The dog was licking my face.

I stood up and brushed myself off. It was dawn. The sun was barely over the horizon. Strangely enough, I heard sirens. It must have been the ambulance service doing a drill or something.

I wondered how I could get into the house and what I would tell Mum when she asked why I hadn't slept at Becky's. I crept around the back. The screen door was unlocked. I felt nauseated. It came on suddenly. I slapped my hand across my mouth and ran out into the garden and hurled. I was so never ever drinking again as long as I lived.

I crept inside and made my way to my room. I curled up on my bed and prayed my head would stop thumping. Everything was better when I closed my eyes.

When I woke up again, Mum was standing over me. 'I know you didn't sleep at Becky's last night,' she said. Her voice sounded strange. I expected her to be angry, but she didn't sound it. 'Get dressed, Edwina, and come out to the kitchen. I need to tell you something.' She sounded really serious.

I showered and got dressed. My skull was still thumping, but not quite as severely as before. I headed into the kitchen. Dad was standing there, too. I knew something was wrong.

'Anne-Marie died last night,' Mum said.

I blinked. I thought I was hearing things.

'Do you want to sit down?' Dad asked.

I barely nodded and slumped weakly into the kitchen chair. I couldn't believe it. Anne-Marie had finally succeeded in starving herself to death.

'It was suicide, they think,' my mum said.

'Suicide?'

George and Matthew came screaming from the living room, chasing one another with toy water pistols. Matthew shrieked as George offloaded a round, hitting him in the back.

'I told you boys, not inside!' Mum yelled. The shrillness of her voice made my head throb harder.

'Roberta Himlich said it was suicide,' Dad said. Roberta played tennis doubles with my dad. I remember her saying that, being an ambulance officer in a small town, nine times out of ten you know the victim.

'What?' I couldn't believe it. Nothing was really sinking in. 'She ... How ... When ...?'

George and Matthew seemed to notice our conversation and stopped to listen.

'Well, they don't know for sure yet, but they think it happened some time during the night,' my dad explained.

'She made a real mess,' said Mum.

'Mary ...' Dad said, shaking his head at her.

'Well, she did, Shaun! Roberta said it was a complete mess ...'

'You don't really need to go *there*, Mary,' he said, a disapproving tone in his voice. 'A girl is dead, Mary. Doesn't that mean anything to you? What if it was *your* daughter?'

'Dead, dead, dead ...' George started chanting and dancing about the house. 'Dead as dead as dead can get ...'

'Shut up, George!' I screamed, standing up. 'Shut the hell up, you little—'

'Edwina!' Mum shouted. 'That's enough!' George burst into tears and ran from the room.

'I'm calling Becky!' I said, grabbing the phone from the hand set.

'I don't know if that's a good idea right now,' my father said, gently taking the phone from my hand. 'She probably isn't ready to talk just yet.'

Tears poured down my face. Tears of sheer disbelief. I couldn't believe Anne-Marie would do this. Why would she go that far? I thought she just desperately wanted to be thin. I thought she would get better. I thought this was just a phase. Her own mother had said she couldn't keep this up for long. And now she was dead!

'I think you should go have a rest, Eddie.' he said, wiping my tears away and gently steering me in the direction of my room. 'You probably need some more sleep.'

I heard my mum saying as I left, 'I wonder when the funeral is? What do you think I should bake for the wake, Shaun? I think I'll call Reverend Lockhardt and ask if there is anything I can do. They'll probably need a few volunteers to serve afternoon tea following the service.'

CHAPTER 16

It seemed the entire population of Wattleton had turned up for Anne-Marie's funeral. Becky's parents had chosen to hold it by the graveside at the cemetery. The gusty wind blew dried leaves across the hillside and whipped them up, swirling the colourful display around the legs of the townspeople and the scattered headstones that lined the hill. The trees struggled to stand tall, their branches creaking and swaying back and forth restlessly. The women in the crowd kept a firm hand on their hats. It was eerily quiet for such a large crowd of people, with only low, muffled whispers filling the air. Everyone was respectfully quiet for Becky's family.

It had been a week since Anne-Marie's death. I hadn't seen Becky or even spoken to her. I had tried to call once, on the Friday. Her Uncle Robert had apparently travelled all the way from England as soon as he heard the news. When he answered the phone he said Becky wasn't up to talking. I wanted so badly just to hug her, just to tell her I cared.

At school, the teachers had gone into overdrive, contacting the city authorities about ordering counselling services for anyone who needed it. An assembly was called and the school principal, Mr Fosdike, talked about teen suicide and how it was an event that had rocked the school's foundations. He said Anne-Marie had been a wonderful student—a kind and giving girl—and that she was a high achiever in all her subjects and was destined for great things.

It's a load of crap how people say nice things about you when you're dead. Like they couldn't say it to you when you were alive. Everyone knew that Anne-Marie had starved herself for months on end, and that she'd been caught puking in the toilets at recess before she had finally been confined to home. He forgot to mention that part. He also forgot to mention how, before she was attacked, she regularly skipped classes and was once caught drawing graffiti in the girls' loos and was suspended. He seemed to forget lots of things.

I stood on the hill wearing my black dress with my white lace-up boots. I stared down at them and wished I had more than one pair of good shoes. I clutched a bunch of white daisies from our garden. My dad put his hand on my back and rubbed it up and down. I shook him away. I didn't really like being touched. It gave me the creeps. Mum kept a keen eye on Becky's family as they walked silently up the pathway towards the grave edge.

'They look like they haven't slept in days,' Mum whispered, shaking her head with a sympathetic expression. 'And Becky's mother's hair ... it's so lifeless ... the poor woman obviously hasn't been to the salon ...'

I felt like screaming at her, *Well, what the hell do you expect? Would you sleep if I had topped myself? Would you head straight to the hairdresser for a new do?*

I watched Becky. Her hair was tied back neatly with a thick blue ribbon. She held a small pink teddy bear in her trembling hand. Tears cascaded down her face as she approached the grave. She stood tall, staring straight ahead. Her eyes didn't wander to the deep hole that had been freshly dug for Anne-Marie's coffin. Someone came forward from the crowd and caught Becky's mother just as she stumbled, her legs giving out from beneath her. Becky's dad's face was like cold stone. His lips pressed tightly together, he held his wife's arm and helped her to the white plastic chairs that had been positioned for the family to sit in at the graveside.

Reverend Lockhardt began the service. He spoke as loudly as he could but his voice drifted off, carried away by the wind. We were so far back in the crowd I could barely hear his words. I heard him say something about Anne-Marie's troubled soul having been set free and that she would suffer no more pain from the demons that had besieged her, that the Lamb of God had welcomed her to His flock and she would be blessed with eternal life.

The wind swept up, the clouds above us hanging like an ominous blackened ceiling. I wondered what would happen if the rain broke through and filled Anne-Marie's grave. What would they do then? Would they still lower the casket into the cold, wet ground? Would they get down in there with shovels and attempt to empty it of the water? Would everyone run for cover and leave Anne-Marie's coffin alone in the rain?

I noticed Joey Parsons and Brody Hillbank standing in the distance. They were all dressed up in their best sports jackets. They kept their heads down and hands together. I wondered if they'd been as shocked as I was by Anne-Marie's death. Perhaps they'd sat around laughing about our joyride in the car, about how they'd failed to score with Edwina Saltmarsh. I suddenly remembered Brody's words, *I know,* in relation to Tom. I'd been so consumed with the shock of Anne-Marie's death I hadn't really thought about what had happened, or about Tom. I realised Tom must have bragged to those boys. He must have said something. Why else would Brody have said that? I surveyed the crowd, but I couldn't see Tom. It was a big secret, yeah sure, until it suited him to brag about it.

At the end of the service the townsfolk of Wattleton formed a long line to go up and pay their respects to the family. I joined the line and watched the people ahead of me one by one solemnly hug Becky and her parents, whispering in their ears, patting their backs. Then it was my turn. I'll never forget the strength of Becky's hug. It was as if she tried to draw all my strength and make it hers. How frail and thin she seemed as she cried in my arms. How her eyes seemed completely vacant when she looked at me, as if the world she lived in no longer made sense to her.

Mum hugged Becky's mum and said she felt terrible for her loss, that she couldn't imagine what it must be like to lose a child. She said that God had a plan in all things and this was just part of His plan for Becky's family. She added that she had baked an apple blueberry pie for the wake, and she hoped Mrs Cooper got a piece. Mrs Cooper looked at my mum as if she were completely mad, but then simply nodded and thanked her for her kind words.

I placed the daisies by the graveside. I looked at the coffin. I couldn't connect with the idea that inside lay Anne-Marie's body and that I would never see her again. My best friend had lost her sister. I had not been close to Anne-Marie, but I felt the loss. Why did she take it so far? Why did she have to do this?

Why?

I had no answer.

Only Anne-Marie knew.

CHAPTER 17

Becky dropped around briefly the day after the funeral and told me her mum had decided they needed to get away for a while. Becky's Aunt June, who lived out of town, had invited them to come and stay, and she was going to drive the three of them to her house. Becky said she would call when they got back.

'Can you water the plants while we're away? Mum thought maybe you could feed Imelda as well?'

'Sure.'

'Here's the key.' She passed me a key ring with a photo of Becky on one side and a photo of Anne-Marie on the other.

'The cat food is in the top of the pantry. Imelda likes her rubber ball as well—if you can play with her for maybe five minutes or something. I hate leaving her.'

'Sure. That's no problem.'

'Well, I'd better go. Aunty June said the 'roos will be out when it gets dark, so we have to leave soon.'

'Okay.' I stopped just short of saying, *Have a good time.*

Becky cried again. I gave her another hug. She forced a smile and, appearing stronger for a moment, said goodbye while she could still get the words out.

When Becky arrived home a few weeks later, and I went round to see her, I noticed something was different. I couldn't expect things to be the same, I guess, but there was definitely something else going on.

Becky was standing at the fridge.

'Becky, please don't stand there with the door open. You're letting all the cold air out.' Mrs Cooper said, as she stood by the stove poking whatever she was cooking with a skewer.

The fridge stayed open. Becky didn't budge.

'Becky, please.' Mrs Cooper sighed as she put the lid back on a saucepan.

'I'm looking for something,' Becky said defiantly, fiddling with a jar inside the fridge door.

Mrs Cooper stood with her hands on her hips and said in a firm voice, 'Shut the door *now,* Becky!'

'Whatever!' Becky shouted as she slammed it. I heard glass clanking and rattling inside. Something sounded like it smashed.

'Come on, Ed. Let's get out of here,' Becky said, striding past me out of the kitchen.

'Take your jacket,' Mrs Cooper said. 'It's getting cold.'

Becky ignored her and marched outside.

'See you, Mrs Cooper,' I said politely, and followed Becky out, closing the door quietly behind me.

I caught up with Becky, who was charging along at lightning speed. We walked up the road together in silence. I pulled my jacket tightly around me. Becky lit a cigarette.

'So how are you?' I said, trying to break the ice.

'Screwed up,' was Becky's reply. She took a heavy drag and held the smoke in, finally expelling it through her nose.

I waited for her to say something—anything—but she didn't.

Finally I said, 'Is there something you want to talk about, Bec? Well you know, I mean, I know Anne- Marie—'

Becky cut me off. 'Yeah—my parents are psychos,' she said.

'Join the club,' I said, trying to joke, but she wasn't laughing. 'What makes you say that?'

'Since I found out something when we were away together.'

'Oh?'

'I'm not supposed to tell anyone.'

I wanted to say *You can tell me*, but I didn't want to pressure her. She'd been through a lot in the last few weeks. 'That's okay. I understand.'

Becky stopped on the roadside and took a deep breath, dropping her cigarette and twisting it with her sandshoe. She turned to me and grasped me by the shoulders. 'Can I tell you?' she asked, searching my eyes for a response.

'Anything, Becky. You know we're friends. I'd never say anything you didn't want me to.'

After a long pause she finally said, 'I know why my sister killed herself. I know why she was sick, you know, throwing up and stuff.'

I stood there confused—what did she mean she knew? We all knew—it was because she'd been attacked—it was because Anne-Marie just couldn't cope any longer.

Becky examined my face. 'They told me,' she said.

'Who told you? Told you what?'

'My parents.'

'Uh-huh.' I still wasn't getting it—they knew too, didn't they?

'They knew something I didn't. They knew something about Anne-Marie and her attack that no one else in this town knew.'

'They knew what?' I said, staring at her.

'They knew the whole time,' Becky said, shaking her head, tears welling in her eyes.

'Knew what, Becky? You're not making any sense.'

'They knew who attacked my sister. They knew who it was that dragged her into the car.'

'What?' I didn't know what to say. We kept walking. 'I don't understand—they knew and they didn't have him arrested? Who was it, Becky?'

'Something happened to her ...' Becky said. 'Something unspeakable.'

'What? What happened?' I asked. Becky paused for a moment and looked around, checking for anyone who might have been within earshot.

'Do you remember my Uncle Norman, my dad's brother?' Becky finally asked.

Uncle Norman? Vaguely. I'd met him once or twice. I didn't think he lived in Wattleton—I didn't know where he lived. I suddenly realised he hadn't been at the funeral. Why was she asking me about her Uncle Norman?

'Do you?' she prompted.

'Um, yeah. I think I met him once, a long time ago, though, Bec. Probably years and years ago.'

'Well, before the um ... before the attack at the oval ...' Her voice trailed off. There was that strange silence once again.

'Yeah? Bec?'

'Okay, Eddie. You have to promise. You have to swear to God you never ever tell another living soul, okay? Make the most excellent promise you can make, Ed.'

'Okay, okay. I do. I promise.'

'God, Edwina. It's so completely gross.' She took yet another deep breath and then spoke the words quickly. 'He stayed at our house a few times, Uncle Norman,' Becky continued, 'years ago on his way home, up north. Some time during the night he crept into Anne-Marie's room.'

'Your parents told you this?' I said, feeling prickles rising on the back of my neck.

'Oh God, it's so completely bloody disgusting, Ed. You have no idea.'

'What happened?' I asked, already convinced I didn't want to know.

'Well, apparently Anne-Marie woke up from her sleep to find him on top of her ... You know, like touching her ...' She was still speaking quickly, shaking her hands at her sides as if she was trying to rid herself of something filthy.

I didn't answer. I felt cold all of a sudden.

'Of course she didn't know it was Uncle Norman to begin with because the room was so dark. I have a night light, but Anne-Marie doesn't, or didn't.' She took another deep breath. 'Anyway, she was too paralysed with fear to scream, and he just kept touching her, and finally, apparently, after some time, she got the guts to speak up, to ask who was there in the room with her. He told her it was him.'

'He told her?' I asked weakly.

'Yes, he told her, and she told him to stop and to get out of her room. But he didn't stop, Ed. He did things to her ... sick things ...' Becky started crying. 'Can you believe it? And in the morning she told my mother.'

'She told her?'

'Yeah. Mum went off at the old bloke and told him to get out. Mum told Dad, but he didn't believe her. Dad said Mum had never liked my Uncle Norman, and Anne-Marie was exaggerating. He said Uncle Norman probably just kissed her on the cheek and she took it the wrong way. Anyway, Mum kicked Uncle Norman out and told him never to bother coming back to our house again. And he didn't ... Well, at least not until ...'

The penny dropped. 'It was him? It was your Uncle Norman? At the old oval?'

'Dad wanted to see him. Dad and Mum had this massive fight over it and Mum told him he could see his brother as long as he didn't come to the house. They met at the pub for a beer. I guess Uncle Norman spotted Anne-Marie walking home from school when he was on his way home and decided to finish what he'd started. He was the one who raped her.'

Raped. My head whirled until I felt like I needed to sit down, my legs growing weak beneath me.

'I know, I know, it's hard to believe,' Becky said. 'Dad threatened to leave if anyone found out. My parents told Anne-Marie not to tell anyone, not even me. They told her if they never spoke to Uncle Norman or saw him again it would all go away just like it never happened. Dad said if they told anyone, the police would haul Uncle Norman off to gaol and he'd never see the light of day ever again. They said Grandma wouldn't survive the shock.'

'Jesus.'

'They said in a small town like this, they had no choice. They said Dad would be looked at strangely—that he wouldn't be allowed to coach the netball again because the people might think he was capable of the same thing as his brother. You know how it is. Anne-Marie would be an outcast if everyone knew. They just wanted her to be normal, to have normal relationships—get married, stay in Wattleton and have children. She couldn't do any of those things if people knew the truth. My parents wouldn't be able to live normally in this town any more if people knew—every time they stepped out of the house to do anything, people would be whispering about them. They said they were doing it to protect me, too.'

'But it wasn't her fault,' I said. Would the people of Wattleton really treat Anne-Marie like it was her fault? Like she enjoyed it or something?

'That's why she was throwing up all the time, Ed.'

I didn't understand.

'You know ... She was trying to get him out of her—out of her system, out of her mouth—out of her body. She was trying to find some control—something she had control over.'

My mind suddenly flashed to the night I had thrown up the fruit.

'And in the end she couldn't rid herself of him,' Becky gasped. 'It should be him, Ed! It should be Uncle Norman lying in the ground.'

Poor Anne-Marie. Under the cold ground of the cemetery, lying in the pitch black dark in a box where no one would ever touch her again.

'The bastard, the dirty incestuous old man. I mean, it could have just as easily been me, Ed. What if he'd come into *my* room? He could have chosen me but he chose her—chose her to rape.'

I hated her using that word.

There was silence between us. I struggled to absorb what Becky had told me. Maybe if Anne-Marie had fought harder—maybe if she'd screamed and called out for help, it would have ended.

'Did they fight?' I asked quietly.

'Fight?' Becky said, looking totally confused. 'What do you

mean, *Did they fight*?'

'I mean, did she struggle with him or hit him—try to scream, try to escape?'

Becky was staring at me like I was some kind of stranger. You could see her face reddening. Finally she spat, 'What do you think, Edwina? That she wanted it? That because she didn't escape with a broken nose or bruises, or his skin under her nails, that it wasn't rape? That she wasn't terrified? That he wasn't older and larger than her and could smash her face with one fist? She said the word *No,* for God's sake! You think this was somehow her fault?'

I thought of Tom's fist hitting the car door that night at Arcoona Creek. 'No.'

'Do you think she wanted it?'

'No.'

'Well then, it's rape.'

We stood there staring at each other.

Bec started shaking her head at me. 'I thought you were my friend, Ed.'

'I am.'

'Well, you don't seem to believe what I'm telling you.'

'No, that's not it.'

'Oh, and I suppose you think my parents keeping it a secret was the right thing to do, hey?' she said sarcastically, her hands on her hips, her face screwed up with anger.

I didn't answer her. In a town like this, maybe it was.

'I'll take that as a yes, then, shall I?' Becky shouted at me, and spun on her heel, going back up the road. 'Some friend you are! Some friend! Don't bother calling me, Ed. Just go back to your perfect little world will you? Just rack off!'

I went to call out to her but her back was already turned. The back of her hand was up in the air, signalling to me like a stop sign.

Stop. Give it up. Let it go.

If only I could.

CHAPTER 18

My family ate lamb chops, watching the six o'clock news.

'Edgar Hollingarth was gaoled today by the Supreme Court of New South Wales for the statutory rape of a thirteen-year-old Sydney girl. In sentencing, Justice Angus Rosalind said that Hollingarth was a man who had displayed little remorse for his actions during the trial. He had preyed on the kind nature of the girl's parents to secure their trust before carrying out the brutal rape of their daughter on several occasions. Justice Rosalind said thirty-two-year-old Hollingarth's actions were disgraceful, and that his victim would endure a lifelong legacy of psychological and physical trauma.'

'Why is that man going to gaol?' George asked with a mouth full of mashed potato.

'That's not for boys your age to worry about. Eat your dinner,' Mum said, spearing a lamb chop and sawing away at it furiously with her steak knife.

'Why?' George said.

'Because it's not!' Mum insisted, pointing her knife at him.

I always thought adults told you it was rude to point your knife.

There was silence.

'What does the statutory part mean?' I asked, keeping my eyes firmly on my dinner plate.

Mum almost choked on her food. Putting her cutlery down, she calmly folded her napkin on the table and then put her hands in her lap. She looked at my dad.

'Well,' Dad said slowly, looking cautiously towards my mother, 'it's when an adult person sleeps with a person who is under age. That's against the law.'

'Under what age?' I asked, keeping my eyes directed squarely at my dinner plate.

'Under sixteen, I think. Is it sixteen, Mary?' Dad said, turning to my mum.

'Oh! Honestly, Shaun!' my mum spat at him, picking up her cutlery and attacking her second lamb chop with extra effort.

I felt like saying, *Slow down, Mum, it's already dead. You don't have to kill it a second time.*

'Why do we have to discuss something so distasteful at dinner?' She turned to glare at me. 'Edwina, this is not the kind of conversation to have at dinner, let alone in front of your brothers. Please just hurry up and eat, will you? I want to get the dishes done and then call Reverend Lockhardt about the floral display for this Sunday. I have a lot to organise, you know. These things don't organise themselves.'

Under the age of sixteen. Tom was an adult. Tom was twenty-five.

I was fourteen when Tom had ...

I pushed my lamb chop around my plate with my fork. Suddenly Becky's voice was echoing in my ear. *She said no, didn't she? Well, that makes it rape.*

I'd said no.

Edgar Hollingarth was going to gaol for having sex with a thirteen-year-old girl. I had been fourteen. Anne-Marie had said no to her uncle but he did as he pleased anyway.

Time stood still.

Tom was *my* Edgar Hollingarth.

Tom was *my* Uncle Norman.

I was the Sydney girl on the news.

I was Anne-Marie.

Time started again.

So did the ticking of my secret time bomb.

CHAPTER 19

Edwina,' Ms Landy said after art class on a Tuesday afternoon, 'can you stay back a moment? I'd like to discuss something with you.'

'Sure,' I answered, looking over my shoulder at Becky, who was walking out the door. Another day had passed and we hadn't spoken, not even so much as looked sideways at one another. There she was, walking out the door with Hayley, and another chance was gone. My heart ached. I missed my best friend. I would give anything to explain to Becky and to make her understand. I'd never felt as alone as I did right now.

When everyone had left the room, Ms Landy closed the door quietly behind them. When she pulled down the blind on the glass panel I immediately knew something was wrong. What exactly I had done, I couldn't think of. I didn't remember being late. I certainly wasn't talking in class. I thought I had handed up all of my assignments?

'Sit down, Edwina.'

I took a seat. Ms Landy carefully drew up a stool and sat opposite me. Her face was drawn and serious. *Here goes*, I thought. *I'm about to cop it.* It's usually best, in my experience, to be prepared. That way you have some excuses lined up. Unfortunately, this time I didn't have a clue what it was about.

'I've been wanting to have a quiet talk with you, Edwina.' Ms Landy said. She ran her paint-stained hand through her silky blonde hair and then rested it on the art folder that sat on the table between us. Ms Landy was a pretty woman, perhaps in a bohemian, artsy-fartsy sort of way. She was wearing a big tortoiseshell necklace and a colourful crochet scarf, which I'm telling you were not in fashion according to *Dolly*. But Ms Landy had this weird self-assured style about her, and that didn't seem to matter.

'Edwina, a few of your teachers have noticed that you seem a bit distracted lately. Your grades are dropping, which is unusual for you, considering you are normally a very good student.'

I stared at her blankly. I hadn't realised my grades were that bad.

'Is there something bothering you? Something you want to talk about?' She tucked a strand of hair behind her ear and looked at me expectantly.

I looked down at the table, immediately uncomfortable. With my two pointer fingers, I traced the edge, focusing intently on the thin black line of the white laminate. I ran my fingers lightly along it, not daring to look up. *Something I want to talk about*, she said. I could probably write a whole book on what I wanted to talk about—trouble was, there wasn't much I could say out loud.

'Look, Edwina. I must admit, there are some other ... well, other ... indications—Yes, that's the right word—that have made me want to have this talk with you.'

Ms Landy was opening the art folder. She was pulling out pages and pages of artwork. I was shocked to see they were all mine—sketches I'd done in class and some I'd done for homework. I thought they had been assessed already. She spread the drawings out over the table. 'Edwina, do you notice something about your portraits?'

I looked at them. There was the one of my dad, the one I'd completed the night Tom had first kissed me. There was the one of George, who had posed for me. One of Becky. A few of other students in the class, and one of Frau Wassarwitz that I'd drawn during German class one day when I'd been bored out of my brain with singing 'O, Tannenbaum'. I shook my head.

'Well,' Ms Landy said, leaning over the pictures, 'all of these portraits, bar the one of your father, are missing their mouths.'

I paused and surveyed the drawings. She was right. So I

couldn't draw a mouth. So I didn't like drawing mouths. I sucked at it—so what? What was the big deal?

'Why didn't you draw a mouth on these portraits?'

I shrugged. 'I don't know. I just like them that way.'

Ms Landy took a deep breath. 'You like them that way?'

'Yeah.'

There was a heavy pause.

'Is there something you want to talk about, Edwina?' Ms Landy asked tentatively. 'Something you feel you can't talk about—to anyone?'

I sat there silently, a little taken aback. All this fuss from rotten grades and some stupid drawings? Paranoia took hold. Did she know something? Who else knew?

'I'm not sure,' I said finally.

'Not sure you want to talk, or not sure you know what's wrong?'

'Not sure I want to talk.'

The room was deafeningly quiet. I could hear nothing but the clock ticking on the wall. The afternoon sun coming through the huge windows bathed the room in bright yellow light. Papier-mâché creations dangled above us, moving ever so slightly with the artificial breeze of the air conditioning. Technicoloured children's art lined the walls or rested half finished on easels. Pots of paint lined the benches and unwashed paintbrushes piled on top of one another overflowed on to the wash-up sinks, turning the water a dirty grey colour.

'You don't need to be afraid. Your hands are shaking,' she said.

So they were.

'Why are you drawing portraits of people without mouths? Does it make you feel something?' she persisted.

Though I couldn't look at her, I could feel her concerned blue eyes evaluating my face, waiting for some kind of giveaway answer. I didn't know what to say or how to explain it. After some time, I simply nodded.

'What? How do you feel?'

'I don't know. It makes me feel ... good,' I answered quietly.

'Feel good?' Ms Landy asked, sounding slightly surprised.

I nodded again.

Ms Landy let out a long sigh. I could feel her eyes still trained on me, trying to drill inside for the truth. 'Edwina?'

'Ed. Everyone calls me Ed.'

'Okay, Ed. Look, whatever you tell me ... Well, you can trust me. I wouldn't judge you.'

I dared to glance at her. Maybe this was my chance. Maybe I could talk to her.

'Is it your parents?'

An imaginary buzzer went off in my head. On a scale of one to one hundred, she'd just scored fifty points. Yes, it was my parents. When wasn't it my parents? My mum and all her stupid church stuff; my dad, who never took anything seriously. That was only the beginning. I couldn't find the words to explain enough, so I didn't bother.

'Is it someone else? At school, maybe?'

Seventy points. Becky. Becky who thinks I don't believe her story, who thinks I betrayed our friendship, who thinks I don't understand. Kylie Baxter & Co, who walked around with their noses in the air and looked down at the nobodies like me. Joey Parsons, Brody Hillbank, Matty Rogers and their gutless mates.

'Outside of school?'

Eighty-five points. Maybe I should tell her it was the whole world. It was my parents, it was Becky, it was Tom. It was my place in the world and where I fitted, if I fitted at all, which I had seriously begun to doubt. What was Ms Landy going to do about it if I told her, anyway—fix it? Like you can turn back the clock. What was the point in talking at all? What's done is done—that's what my father always tells my mother when she's going completely nuts over something she's screwed up. No point in stressing about it. Just get on with it.

'Has someone hurt you?'

One hundred points: dancing lights, shooting skyrockets, buzzers and ringing bells. You get the prize, Ms Landy—trip for two around the world, all expenses paid. Go home now. Show's over.

'Is someone making you feel unsafe?'

Crap. This woman didn't give up, did she? Didn't she get the fact that no words could explain how I felt? Did she honestly think I was going to tell her about everything? About Tom?

'Look,' Ms Landy said, sounding more than a little frustrated, 'I'm convinced, having got this far in our talk, that there is something bothering you. I suspect it's fairly major. If you're not going to tell me what it is, then I'm going to have to tell you, I am not giving up until you do tell me. I think you have so much potential, Ed. I can't sit by and watch you ... Well, watch you drifting like this. You have to tell me that you are—at the very least—all right.'

I couldn't tell her that even.

'So you're not all right,' she said.

I could feel the hot waves of tears just there in the background, threatening to break through. I wanted to scream at her to guess; just hurry up and guess—read my mind and figure out what was wrong so I didn't have to say it out loud. She looked so perplexed, I realised she wasn't even close. And God, I needed the help of someone.

'I think ...' I started to say.

'What, Ed?'

'I think I may have ...' I stopped again. I looked up at the clock, the second hand ticking away, headed back to the twelve. Would it go another round, or was I about to call time? 'This guy ... um ...'

'A guy?'

'He ... um ...'

'Did he hurt you?'

I didn't answer. I stared out the window. I saw pine trees. I saw tall, dark green pine trees lined up like soldiers at the edge of a battlefield, poised on the brink, about to fall forward. Suddenly I was running through the trees, over the dead pine needle carpet, disappearing into the darkness ... running, running. Running away.

'How? How did he hurt you?' Ms Landy's quiet, gentle voice seemed to call out to me. 'What did this guy do?'

She was asking questions again. I shrugged. I could let her guess now.

'Did he hit you?'

I shook my head. 'No, he didn't hit me.'

'How old is this guy?'

'I don't know ... Older ... I think, like twenty-five, maybe?'

Ms Landy picked up a paintbrush from the desk behind her and held it firmly, repeatedly running a single finger through the bristles. This time she wasn't looking at me when she asked, 'Did he touch you?'

I didn't answer her. *Touch*? Like the touch of his fingers on my cheek, stroking it, tucking my hair behind my ears? *Touch* didn't go far enough to explain it. The way his fingertips dug into my breasts; the way his strong arms held me down; the way his voice echoed in my ear the voice of some evil dictator—*Do what I tell you to do ... Don't speak ... Just shut up and do it ... You'll like it ... I promise you ... Just let me touch you like this ... Why aren't you feeling something?... What's wrong with you? Other girls like this—why don't you?*

'Ed?'

I bit down hard on my bottom lip. Silence was an admission, wasn't it? My ticking time bomb was about to be detonated.

'How many times?' Ms Landy said quietly. She put the paintbrush on the table between us and reached for my hand. She caught it just before I managed to pull away. She held on to it tightly, refusing to let me go.

I shrugged. I didn't really remember clearly. I remembered the start of so many times with Tom, but not necessarily the end. Pieces that didn't fit together, like one of those frustrating giant jigsaw puzzles that send you mental trying to work them out.

'Sweet Jesus.' She released my hand and covered her open

mouth. Leaning on one elbow, she stared out the window, her eyes wide and blinking slowly. 'Did he rape you?' she asked, turning back to me.

BOOM! Detonation. Silence. Shock. Disbelief.

'Who is this person?' Ms Landy demanded.

I pressed my lips tightly together. Who was he? He was the demon that I would never be free from. He filled my head, consumed my thoughts, crawled just under the surface of my skin and made it ripple with fear any time anyone touched me. He was inside my throat, choking my words, constricting how much of life I breathed in and fiercely guarding how much I gave back. I was riddled with him like a bad apple all the way to the core—rotten and crawling with dirty, disgusting maggots.

'I'm the first person you've told this to?' Ms Landy asked. 'Would you consider telling your parents?'

'No!' I said loudly. The anger in my voice punctured the air that hung thickly between us. The clock sounded as if it were ticking out of time. Imagine telling Mum! Lord only knows what she would do. It would probably wind up being all about her, anyway. About how it wasn't her fault, about how bad she felt. About how useless my dad was for not knowing his friend would do this. How the whole town would know what a terrible mother she was. It wouldn't be about me and how I felt.

'I haven't told you anything, Ms Landy. If you noticed, I haven't answered you.' I said defiantly.

There was yet another long silence.

'Ed, I'm a school teacher. That means I'm a mandatory reporter. Do you know what that means?'

'No.'

'It means that I have to report this to the authorities.'

I panicked. Oh God, no! What authorities? Just leave me alone.

'I haven't said anything.' Who was I kidding? My unspoken words had spoken the loudest.

Ms Landy searched my eyes and turned away to look out the window.

'Have you considered that you might not be the only girl this man has abused? What if there are others? What's to stop him trying it again if he gets away with what he did to you?'

'I don't know what you're talking about.'

She turned back towards me and, looking into my eyes, seeing completely though my façade, she went on. 'No one would hold you responsible for that, Ed. *He*'s responsible. He's older than you, right? He should know better. He should know the law. What he did was wrong, and he probably knows that. I'm just saying he might try this again.'

We sat there staring at each other, the clock ticking.

'Ms Landy, what are you going to do?' I finally asked.

'I'm not sure, really.'

'Ms Landy, I don't care what you think you know. The truth is, I haven't said anything to you. I'd just tell people you're lying. You don't even know his name.'

Ms Landy, unmoved by my threats, asked, 'So, you're prepared to shoulder this yourself?'

What were my choices in a town like Wattleton, honestly? Maybe Becky didn't see her parents' logic, but I did. It wouldn't be Tom who'd be frowned on. It'd be me. Me for letting him kiss me. Me for wanting to have an older boyfriend. Me for flirting with him. Me for wearing outfits that made him want to touch me. Me for not telling my parents when he first came into my room. It was all my fault.

'Don't you want something to happen to him, though, for what he's done to you?'

'I don't know right now.' That was the truth. I didn't know what I wanted to happen to Tom. The only person worth punishing right now was me.

Ms Landy looked at her watch. 'Ed, I'll have to report this.'

I didn't comment. She looked squarely at me, obviously digesting the fact that I was resolute in saying nothing.

'Do you know that men rely on this?' she asked.

'What?'

'This.'

'What?' What the hell was she on about?

'The code of silence.'

I didn't understand.

She said it again. 'The code of silence, Ed. They do this—abuse you, rape you, whatever—and then they rely on the fact you won't say anything to anyone because you're too embarrassed. Too ashamed.'

I thought of Tom's words—*This will be our secret.*

'Okay. Look. I'm not making promises,' she said. 'You're obviously not ready to deal with this ... I think you need some time. I'm going to have to report this, Ed—soon. It's probably unorthodox, but I'd like a chance to talk with you again before I do. I think it will give you some time to get used to the idea.'

'Soon?' How long did she mean? I should never have opened my fat mouth. I didn't want to talk to anyone. I could hardly talk to her. What the hell made her think I'd talk to anyone else? What would happen when they told my parents? Because I bet they would. As if I'd talk to my parents about this!

'How can anyone help, Ms Landy?' There was no way to help me. I could see that clearly—why couldn't she?

'Counselling, maybe. I don't know yet.' She was placing my artwork back in the folder. 'You'd better go home now.'

'Okay,' I said, easing myself down from the stool and picking up my bag.

'You're my best student. I care a lot for you. You have so much potential, Ed,' she said, placing her hand on my shoulder and staring meaningfully into my face. Her kind words ricocheted off the protective invisible bubble that had formed around me. The one that let nothing good in and kept all the bad stuff locked safely inside.

I nodded. *Yeah, a fat lot of potential,* I thought.

I left the art room and walked, slightly dazed, towards the car park.

My mum was waiting for me. George and Matthew were in

the back seat. She looked crabby. 'You think the whole world waits for you, don't you, Edwina?' she spat sarcastically as I slid myself into the car. 'The sooner you grow up and realise there are other people in the world besides you, the better off we'll all be!'

She reversed out and swung the car backwards. I heard a thump. I knew immediately she'd hit a garden light pole. The boys looked wide-eyed at one another and waited for Mum to explode. She thrust herself out of the car and went around the back to inspect the damage.

'You're in trouble now,' Matthew said. As if I wasn't from the moment I was born.

'This is all your fault, Edwina Maryanne Saltmarsh!' Mum fumed, getting back in the car. She knocked her head against the door frame as she got in. Surprisingly, she slumped over the steering wheel, clutching her head with both hands and rocked from side to side, quietly sobbing. Then, suddenly recharged, she yelled, 'If you weren't late, I wouldn't get angry and then things like this wouldn't happen!'

Of course it was my fault. Everything that happened was my fault. *Everything.*

CHAPTER 20

'Something struck me after we talked the other day, Ed.' Ms Landy was talking to me as she moved tins of coloured pencils, piles of paperwork and books aside on her desk. She hoisted herself up and planted her backside on the wooden desk, which creaked momentarily under her weight. Casually, she crossed her legs and clasped her charcoal-stained hands over one knee, letting one of her blue strappy shoes dangle freely from her toes.

'You're a strong girl to have dealt with this all by yourself for so long.' She eyed me, knowing already how I'd react to such a comment.

'I'm not strong.'

'But you are, Ed. I don't think you know how strong you really are.'

'If I was strong, I wouldn't have let him—'

She cut me off. 'You were strong enough to think you could shoulder this all by yourself—the rape. You think you're strong enough to deal with this alone.'

There was that damned R-word again. Did she think I was stupid? I wasn't going to fall for that *You're so strong to have dealt with this all by yourself* crap—I wasn't strong at all. If I were, I doubted I'd be in this mess.

'Do you think what happened to you was your fault?'

Of course it was. What kind of question was that? 'Why?' I asked her.

'Well, you sound like you're trying to protect everyone out of guilt—like you think this is your fault and somehow you're going to fix it by protecting everyone from the truth—including protecting him.'

'I don't know ...'

'Well?'

'It was my fault.'

'Why do you think that?'

I shook my head. It wasn't up for question in my mind—it was a fact, an unquestionable fact, just like the sky being blue and the grass being green was fact, so it was fact that it had all been my fault. 'It was my fault I wanted him to like me. I thought it was exciting at first.'

'Thought what was exciting?'

'When he started, you know, paying attention to me. I liked it.'

'What do you mean by *paying attention to you*?'

'Oh, um, just like the way he looked at me, the things he said when he mucked around with me ...'

'Mucked around?'

'Yeah, like when he tickled me and stuff ...'

Ms Landy's shoe flopped for the final time and fell on the floor. She didn't seem to mind, and kicked the other shoe off too, revealing her pink-painted toenails. She eased herself off the desk and came over to sit next to me. She looked very serious. 'That's called *grooming*, Ed.'

'I'm sorry?'

'It's called *grooming*. He was testing you.'

Testing me for what? She obviously didn't know what I meant. 'He was flirting with me, Ms Landy,' I said, explaining it to her. 'I flirted with him too, which is one of the reasons it was my fault.'

'No, Ed. Listen to me. He was *grooming* you. I bet when he tickled you, he was testing how far you'd let him go—how much you'd let him touch you—*where* you'd let him touch you. How you'd react, if you liked it. And then he'd probably try a bit more, to see if he could get further. It might have seemed like flirting to you, Ed. In normal relationships, that's what people do, I guess: flirt, say things, tickle or touch one another. That kind of thing could be considered flirting, but when there's an unequal power balance like this—he being so much older than you—it isn't flirting. It's a calculated step in a process, Ed. He was grooming you. He was getting you ready for something else.'

I'm not sure I understood what she was saying. He was doing something I didn't know about? How did Ms Landy know that?

'Ms Landy, how ...?'

'I rang a counsellor friend of mine after I filed a report last night.'

'You filed the report already?'

'I told you, Ed, I have to. I'm required to by law.'

'What did they say? What will they do?' I asked, instantly panicked.

'They have a priority process, Ed. They consider you to be out of immediate danger at the moment and they also know it wasn't a family member who committed the offence. They have referred the matter to the police.'

'No! Ms Landy, you don't understand. I don't want to do anything. I don't want to talk to the police. I want it to go away. I won't tell them anything, I just won't!'

'Ed, I don't mean to scare you. It will probably be a few weeks until the police contact you. I'm not really sure what they'll do from there. They'll probably help you with counselling and give you other information. Ed, it will be okay.'

That was easy for her to say. Why did everything feel like it was snowballing? It just seemed to get worse and worse.

'Ed, because it may be a few weeks until the police speak with you, I'd like to see if I can help. My friend, the counsellor, gave me some valuable information. I'd like to find out a little more, if that's okay?'

I nodded.

'What else did he do, aside from tickle you? Did he kiss you?'

'Yes. I really wanted him to kiss me.' I felt a terrible shame for admitting that. 'I'd never been kissed before.'

'Oh, sweetheart.'

'I thought it was exciting. I thought he might love me. I liked the way that felt, that someone loved me.'

'There's nothing wrong with that, Ed. Every girl wants to be loved, eh? I know I do.'

For some reason, as soon as she said that, I looked at her wedding finger. There was no ring. I wondered why. She was gorgeous. I couldn't believe she might actually be single.

'It's what he wanted from you that was wrong, Ed. You're a schoolgirl, for God's sake, and he's not some schoolboy—he's a man, an adult. He should have known, and probably did know, a whole lot better. Did he tell you not to say anything—I mean about what you and he were doing?'

How did she know that? 'He told me to keep it a secret ... but I think he may have told other people ...'

'What makes you think that?'

'Oh, just something a guy at school said.' I wasn't about to get into what had happened with Joey and Brody. Ms Landy would probably sign me up never to be released if I told her about that as well.

'You think he bragged about it?'

'I don't know. Maybe.' Of course he did. He must have told those boys in the football change rooms. Maybe he even told men his age. I felt the redness climbing my cheeks, colouring my face with the heat of humiliation. I could just imagine the things that would have been said about me.

'How many times did it happen? How many times did he ... rape you?'

'Oh God, Ms Landy, can you not say that ... *that* word?' My stomach knotted itself tightly. I couldn't believe I was hearing that word in connection with me. It wasn't me—it had to be some other girl. Not me. I was finding it hard to breathe. I shifted my weight on the stool and ran my hands nervously over my skirt, smoothing out the creases. I suddenly remembered my game of noughts and crosses on my dress. Then I remembered the chocolate ice-cream stain. Then I remembered the blood.

Ms Landy spoke in a low, soothing voice. She took my hands

and held them still. 'You know, any kind of penetration ... with his fingers or with an object ... If you didn't want it, Ed, that makes it rape. If he did other things, too ... Well, they can be considered rape also.'

Overwhelmed, I felt my chest heaving and I was gulping for air. Tears welled in my eyes, waiting for me to give them permission to fall. I knew if I let them I might lose control. Losing control was what I feared most.

'Ed, I'm not going to ask you for details,' Ms Landy said, lightly squeezing my hand. 'Maybe soon you might have to tell someone like a counsellor—but right now I'm concerned about ... Well, did he use some kind of protection—like a condom?'

'No ... um ... maybe ... I don't really know ...' My voice sounded like someone else's. I pulled my hands away from her. It made me so uncomfortable to be touched. I wondered if I would ever be able to be touched by someone without thinking about it, without feeling that I wanted to run away. 'I'm not sure, really.'

'You might need to get tested, Ed, for sexually transmitted diseases. You could have even fallen pregnant, Ed—did you think of that?'

'No.' That was the truth. Until she said it, the thought hadn't crossed my mind.

Ms Landy looked down and fiddled with her bracelet. Her gaze slipped into the distance, as if she had just been transported miles away. It was a look that slowly resonated with me until I realised it was almost like looking into the bathroom mirror—watching that girl with the vacant eyes. I knew the look. Ms Landy was watching her own story playing in her head, just as I did. It played scenes at random—sometimes with the sound of his voice, but mostly with a kinder, deceitful silence that somehow made it more bearable. Standing on the outside, as if watching yourself from afar, you saw things—terrible things. Watching someone who looked like you, moved like you, spoke like you—but who wasn't you—doing *those* things. Those awful, disgusting things. You wouldn't do *those* things?

You wouldn't let him—you'd stop him, wouldn't you? And then the screen would go blank, leaving you with that familiar sick feeling in the pit of your stomach. I knew that look. Something had happened to Ms Landy, too.

'Ms Landy?'

Ms Landy blinked and softly shook her head. She squeezed my hand hard and smiled—a sad smile. You could tell she knew at that moment she had given her own secret away. After a long silence she asked, 'Do you know they estimate the statistics are something like one in three, Ed? One in three women has been raped, sexually assaulted or molested. Think of all the women you know, Ed—your mother, your grandmother, your friends, your friends' mothers—women on television, women who work in offices.' She paused. 'Even your teachers, Ed … women everywhere. One in three women. You're not alone, Ed.'

'But Anne-Marie …'

'Yes, I know—terrible.' Ms Landy drew a deep breath and shook her head slowly. 'Poor Anne-Marie. That's what happens when girls believe they're alone. Anne-Marie obviously blamed herself—just like you're doing now. Why do you blame yourself, Ed?'

'I think I should have fought him—said more, struggled maybe. I don't know. I was just so confused … and scared.'

'Scared? Maybe you were just smart, Ed, and didn't know it.'

'Smart?' How could I have been smart? Was she crazy?

'Well it's like this, Ed. You were faced with a choice. Self-preservation won out. He might have beaten you, perhaps, if you'd refused him.'

'I don't know.' Would he? Tom, who put his hand on my cheek and called me beautiful. Tom, who smashed his fist down on the car door in frustration at me. Could he have beaten me?

'I was just a stupid little girl who—'

'That's right, Ed. No, not the stupid part, but really, honey, you were a little girl.'

I shook my head. What did she know?

'It's not your fault, Ed.'

'Yes it was. Especially the first time.'

'Why? What could you possibly tell me that would make me think that you'd asked for it?'

'I'd been smoking pot, Ms Landy,' I blurted out, without stopping to think I was revealing this to a school teacher. 'I didn't know what I was doing. He said I didn't know what I was doing ...'

'Did he give you the drug, Ed?' Ms Landy asked calmly. I expected her to be shocked that her best student had smoked pot, but she seemed completely unmoved.

'No. I smoked some with my friends before.'

'Okay. I see.' Ms Landy stood up and started to pace the room with her arms folded across her chest. She stopped and stared out the window for a minute or so before turning back to me. *Now she realises*, I thought. *Now she knows it was my fault. Now she'll see this the way I'm seeing it. She'll understand me now.*

'Ed, I'm not going to pretend to you that I don't know this kind of thing goes on with kids your age. There would be dozens of adults out there ready to condemn what I'm about to say, but as far as I'm aware, they'd rather stick their heads in the sand. The truth is, I know what I got up to when I was your age, and I was no angel—far from it. I imagine you're more than capable of the same sort of behaviour. The fact of the matter is that teenagers try stuff out—especially drugs, alcohol, sex—because it's like participating in some dangerous sport. There's the possibility you could get hurt, but you think nothing bad is going to happen to you—it's all a bit of fun.'

'Yeah,' I said, convinced she understood now.

'But you know what? Yeah, I'm not thrilled you were smoking pot, Ed. But I'd be ignorant if I didn't allow for the chance that at some stage you might try it. And just because you tried it on the day you were raped doesn't make the rape your fault, Ed. Maybe you felt out of control because of the pot, but do you know who was in control? Who was in control the whole time—pot or no pot? He was, Ed. That's right. And frankly, I think he's even more of a monster for taking advantage of you when you were in that state, Ed. You have to listen to me. This isn't your fault, Ed.'

'Yes it was. There was more than one time. I just did what he told me to do, and I don't know why.'

Ms Landy came back over to me and took a seat opposite. 'It's like *role-playing*, Ed. It's a weird thing, and I find it a bit difficult to explain.' She rested her elbows on the table, clasping her hands together. 'You just kind of filled a role with him—like an actor in a play. You had a part. You knew how to play it. For whatever reason—whether it had happened too many times already, or if you were paralysed with fear, or if you weren't prepared to acknowledge what was happening—you kind of just played a role with him. It's like some kind of primal survival instinct, I think. You didn't knowingly do it, Ed. It explains why you said you did what you were told. Something deep inside you was probably telling you to put up with his treatment; that when those incidents took place, when they were over, he'd still be there and you could live out your dream of having an older boyfriend who loved you.'

I felt terribly confused. Was she right? Did I somehow create my reality? It had to be my fault.

'It's not your fault,' Ms Landy said, as if she knew exactly what I was thinking.

No matter how many times it was said to me, I doubted it would ever ring true. 'I let him.'

'You were fourteen. You were a child in real terms. You're—what? Close to sixteen, now? Think about what you know now that you didn't know at fourteen. Think of what you will know at eighteen that you don't know now. You were a child at the time, Ed, dealing with things the way a child would. But you're older now, and soon you'll be an adult yourself—a woman, and you're going to have to deal with it as an adult. This won't leave you, Ed—and you'll need help, perhaps professional help, to deal with it.'

'Ms Landy, I just feel so tired. So tired.' Tears made their way down my cheeks, and I had little energy left to stop them.

'You're tired, Ed, because you've been dealing with this by yourself for so long. There's a lot of power in talking—in releasing things. You'd be amazed how much better you'd feel if you let someone help you.'

'Ms Landy, I don't want to speak to anyone else. Can't I just talk to you?'

'Sweetheart, I'm not qualified. You need someone who can help you understand your feelings—give you methods of dealing with this.'

'But Ms Landy, I don't want my parents to know.'

'They're going to have to know some time, Ed.'

'No, God ... Please, no. I can't deal with that as well right now.'

The bell rang, echoing through the room, spilling out into the corridors where children poured from the school yard back into the building—children with uncomplicated lives and happy families. I heard them lining up outside the art room, their voices chiming and squealing with laughter. I wished I could be just like them again.

'Ed, I have to teach,' Ms Landy said, looking towards the door. 'You'd better get to your next class. I'll see what I can do to organise you some help—okay?'

'Okay.'

'And Ed, you're not alone—remember that. One in three.'

One in three, I thought, leaving the art room. I bet those one in three weren't living in Wattleton.

CHAPTER 21

It was Sunday afternoon. Mum was in a reasonably good mood. Church had gone well, apparently. I had been permitted to stay home by myself for the first time ever—thank God. Well, maybe not thanks to God, as I suppose God would probably prefer I went to church. The reason church had gone so well, according to Mum, was that her vanilla slice made with Sao biscuits had been a real hit with Reverend Lockhardt, who had remarked that God would save a place for my mum in His heavenly kitchen for cooking food as good as that. Mum repeated this comment three times when she arrived home—just in case we didn't hear her the first time. Sometimes I'm convinced God created my mum just to amuse Himself.

I looked through the living room window at her kneeling down in the garden pulling up bulbs.

Dad had the secateurs and was trimming back the rose bushes. Mum wore an enormous sun hat tied with a big yellow bow under her chin. She was, as always, the queen of dag, even in the garden.

I noticed a pile of daisies heaped into a mound beside her. I thought of the daisies I'd put on Anne-Marie's grave. Perhaps I should go visit the cemetery. I hadn't been since the funeral, and it looked as if the daisies were headed for the compost heap anyway.

I was about to step out the door when a familiar-looking red Cortina pulled into the driveway.

Tom's car.

I stood just behind the curtains, my heart pounding. What was he doing here? What did he want? I watched as he climbed out and greeted my mum with a friendly kiss. He was wearing a white T-shirt and track pants that had holes down the side and were covered in splashes of white paint. His black hair was hidden under a baseball cap. He was clutching something—a newspaper.

Something in the car moved and caught my eye. There was a girl sitting in the front seat. Through the curtains and the tinted windows I could make out that she had long dark hair. A cigarette dangled from her fingertips. She leaned forward, adjusted the rear vision mirror and checked her appearance. Suddenly music was blaring—she must have turned up the volume.

Tom was passing my dad the folded-up newspaper. Wiping his brow with the back of his hand, Dad took it, looked down at it and started laughing. He slapped Tom on the back and shook his hand heartily. They appeared to be in raptures over something.

Mum came over and joined them and, oddly enough, planted a kiss on Tom's cheek and hugged him. He kissed her back.

Watching them, I felt waves of nausea. What was he doing? The smug bastard, letting Dad shake his hand and Mum kiss him. If only they knew.

They walked back to the car. The girl hadn't moved. My mum, leaning into the car window, said something to the girl. I heard Tom start the engine. My heart lightened with relief—he was leaving.

My mum and dad stood together, their arms around one another, and waved goodbye.

As Tom left the driveway I watched Mum turn to my dad and clap her gardening-gloved hands together gleefully. Dad leaned down and kissed her cheek, adjusting her hat, and then tapped his finger playfully on her nose. She waved him away, shaking her head, turning back to her gardening.

'Oh, Edwina, you just missed Tom,' she said excitedly as I came out the front door.

I didn't answer.

'He's engaged! Look,' she announced, passing me the

newspaper. My stomach lurched.

I looked at the ad in the classified section of the Wattleton local rag.

'Lisa's from a wealthy farming family in New Zealand. They met on a tour bus. Oh, isn't it wonderful? A wedding! We'll get to go to a wedding! Oh! What will we get for a present?' Mum said, turning to Dad. 'Oh my gosh, I hadn't thought of the expense. We'll need new shoes, you'll need a new suit, Shaun. I'll have to go to the salon ...'

I bent down and picked up the daisies. 'Mum, I thought I might take these, for Anne-Marie's grave.'

She looked at me blankly, and then kneeled back down on the grass. She started digging up bulbs again. 'Shaun,' she continued, ignoring me, 'do you think maybe we could get a babysitter for the boys that night? I mean, I'd really like to just go out and enjoy myself. I haven't been to a wedding in years!'

'Steady on, Mary!' Dad chuckled, slicing the tops of the rose bushes. 'They haven't even had an engagement party yet.'

'Oh! You're right, Shaun! Good grief! That's another present we have to buy. This is going to be very expensive.'

'I'm leaving,' I said, walking out of the driveway. 'I'll be back later.'

Mum looked up at me. 'Where did you say you were going?'

'To the cemetery.'

'Well really, Edwina. I don't see why. She wasn't your friend. Go ahead, though. Don't be long.'

I walked up the road alone, carrying my pathetic little bunch of daisies. Seeing Tom just now was like opening a wound—one that had not even begun to heal. He was real. It *did* happen. I hadn't made it up in my head. He existed for real. How I wished Anne-Marie wasn't dead in the cold, dark ground. I wished I could talk to her, ask her how she felt—tell her she wasn't alone.

At the cemetery, I laid the daisies on the grave and squatted down next to the grey headstone.

'Hi, Anne-Marie. I brought you some flowers.' I propped the flowers up next to the headstone. Several other dried bunches lay alongside, the coloured paper they had been wrapped in bleached by the rain and the sun. 'You must be lonely up here all by yourself. I wanted to come and talk, but I know you can't talk back to me. I hope that you're listening though—that you can hear me. I wanted to tell you that you're not really alone. I mean, well you are now, I guess, but what happened to you ... I know ... and I know how you must have felt. I wish you hadn't killed yourself, Anne-Marie. We could have helped each other. We could have got through this together. Remember Ms Landy? Well, she's explained so much to me—I think something happened to her, too, and she's so right—it does help to talk. It really does.'

'What are you doing here?'

I almost jumped out of my skin. I swung round to see Becky standing there, clearly surprised to see me. She was alone, clutching a posy.

I stood up, brushing myself off and looking back at Anne-Marie's grave. 'I brought some daisies from our garden.'

She eyed me strangely, appearing confused. 'I heard you talking.'

'Oh, I was, um, talking to Anne-Marie. You know, um, saying that we, um, miss her.'

Becky raised an eyebrow. We stared at each other.

'I know you, Edwina Saltmarsh. You're lying.'

I didn't answer.

Slowly, Becky smiled. 'It's good to see you here.'

'Yeah.'

'Want to sit down?'

'Okay.' We sat cross-legged at the edge of Anne-Marie's grave.

'I worry about her up here ... especially at night,' Becky said. 'She was afraid of the dark, you know. More so after ... Well, after Uncle Norman ...'

'Yeah. I know what you mean.' It was ridiculous, really.

Realistically, we both knew Anne-Marie's body was buried way beneath the ground where the sunlight couldn't reach. It was eternally dark down there.

'How are you, Bec? You know—your parents?'

'Oh, we don't really talk that much. My mum's taking some kind of pills the doctor ordered her. She's a bit spacey most of the time. Dad's lost a lot of weight. He's eating, you know, but I think it's just the stress ... and me.' She stared ahead, past Anne-Marie's grave, into the distance. 'I could have helped her, you know. If only I'd asked ... All Anne-Marie had to do was say something—anything. It's too late now to do anything. It's so pointless.'

It was pointless, all right. Anne-Marie's death had achieved nothing but more pain—more people hurting. More people asking questions. More anger. More blame.

'I'm sorry, Becky. That argument we had ...'

She looked at me and slowly shook her head. 'What's wrong with you, Edwina? Something's wrong, isn't it? I've been your best friend for half of your life and I know something has changed you. What's going on? You just reacted so weirdly when I told you. Please tell me what's wrong.'

I looked at her. How could I explain? No one could understand unless I poured out every sordid detail. There would perhaps come a time when I would learn to say the words that frightened me, the words that made everything so real. Speaking those words was accepting that I was raped, and I couldn't deny the truth ever again. I couldn't pretend to be someone else.

'Ed?' Becky nudged me, waiting for a response.

I sat there open-mouthed. I wanted to tell her so badly—for her to understand. The words were on the tip of my tongue. While I didn't speak them, I was in control.

'I ... uh ...' How could I best explain? 'You know your Uncle Norman.'

'Yes,' Becky said.

'Well, what happened to Anne-Marie ... it kind of happened

... to me ...' Tears welled in my eyes. Why wasn't this easier? Why couldn't I just come out and say it? It hurt too much. Would I ever be able to tell anyone and not cringe with fear and shame?

I closed my eyes. 'I think I was ... I know I was ... Well, not just once ... Uh, Tom Atkinson ... He ...'

Becky put out her hand and took mine, clasping it firmly. 'That's why you're here—isn't it?'

I nodded.

'Come here.' She put her arms around me—and for once I didn't flinch. I didn't need to say another word for her to understand. She knew the truth. That *rape* word boxed me, categorised me, and stored me on the shelf with thousands of other women just like me. I didn't want to be part of that group. I couldn't accept it. I never wanted to.

'What is it about these men that makes them think they can do this? I mean, at what point in their lives does someone take them aside and teach them what to do—how to get away with it, what to say? Crap! I tell you what, these bastards need to be hung by their bloody balls.'

I watched the anger colouring her face, the fire raging in her eyes as she spoke.

'I mean, for God's sake! Are they ill-equipped or what? Are their penises so small that they need to prove themselves at every goddamned turn?'

She was belittling my monster. Chopping him down. Making him pathetic.

'What is it?' Becky stood up and screamed up at the heavens, 'What is it, God? Why do these bastards think they can do this to us?'

She looked down at me, her face suddenly lightened. She was like a beautiful angel. 'Come on, Edwina!' Get angry with me! Stand up, girl! Tell the world how you feel!'

I stood up and took her hand. Together, by Anne-Marie's grave, we screamed obscenities towards the sky. Screamed until we were hoarse and could scream no more. I screamed out loud that I hated Tom. I hated him more than I'd ever hated anyone. I hated him for touching me. I hated him for saying he loved me. I hated him for lying to me. I hated him so much I wished he would die. I screamed until my whole body ached. I felt pain, I felt anger, I felt hate—but most of all—I felt me. No longer numb, I reclaimed my body.

We collapsed exhausted, gasping for breath.

'That's for you, sis.' Becky asked, her hand outstretched, tracing the letters on Anne-Marie's headstone with her fingers. She turned to me. 'I won't let him get you, Ed. I won't let Tom do this to you—I just won't. That's a promise you can count on. I'm here for you, Ed.'

CHAPTER 22

'Take this, Edwina,' Mum whispered, passing me a hymn book. 'I want you to sing today. You never sing. You can sing just once for me. So I have something to remember after you leave. I want to remember that my daughter used to sing with me in church.' She had tears in her eyes. 'I love you, Edwina. I'm going to miss you when you go to college.'

I stared at her. My mum. She had been good about the scholarship that Ms Landy had arranged for me at Amberleena College, proud that I had won such an honour. I had heard her bragging to the CWA ladies how proud she was of me. She wouldn't shut up about it. It was embarrassing, but at the same time it felt nice. I knew she would miss me. I could feel it.

Mum looked almost vulnerable. Her thin fingers clasped the hymn book as she gazed up at the cross on the wall. With clarity unlike anything I had ever known, I looked upon her as if she were a child—a fragile child being crushed by the weight of her perception of the world. Mum, who struggled with my father's vagueness and inability to take control of the simplest of things. Mum, who struggled to retain control herself every day of her life.

I looked over at my dad. He was jibing my brothers, hiding their toy cars behind his Bible, laughing quietly and whispering about the goodies for morning tea following the church service. He was oblivious to Reverend Lockhardt, who was calling for the parishioners to turn to John:20.

Mum rolled her eyes at him and breathed a defeated sigh, shaking her head. I had to accept her. She coped how she knew to cope. She wasn't even aware of her own shortcomings. People have to be aware of their faults if they are to accept responsibility for their actions.

My new counsellor, Dr Simone Cartwright, had told me that. I rang her from school every week. Ms Landy and the police had set it up for me. Dr Cartwright worked at a women's counselling centre not far from Amberleena College. When I started there, apparently I could see her in person whenever I needed to.

Ms Landy had turned out to be a pretty cool teacher. She'd done a lot for me, and for that I would always hold her in my heart and be grateful.

Dr Cartwright told me straight off that she wasn't a pill. She said patients came to her looking for a cure. *Fix me*, they'd say. *I want a pill that will make it all go away.* She said I wasn't allowed to ask her to fix me—I had to do that myself. But she'd help me figure out how. She said maybe I would regain strength by talking about what happened with Tom; maybe I would write about my experiences; maybe I would be help others who'd survived rape and sexual abuse. She told me there was hope to heal, but no one else could do it for me. It was up to me, and I would become my own best friend.

I had talked about so much with Dr Cartwright already. I'd not only told her about Tom, but I'd also told her about what happened that night with Joey and Brody, about drinking at Becky's and the car ride afterwards. She says I was lucky I wasn't killed. I didn't really think of that possibility until she said it. She explained that sometimes when you're feeling down on yourself you do destructive things like putting yourself in harm's way. She says she knows I was just angry and I would never make that mistake again. She said some kids only ever got to make that mistake once. Dr Cartwright reckons you're pretty smart if you can learn from your own mistakes—but even smarter if you can learn from someone else's. She said that just like Tom, Joey and Brody knew exactly what they were doing—it was premeditated—and I wasn't to blame for that either. Just because I accepted a ride does *not* mean I accepted anything else.

I told Dr Cartwright about making out with Matty Rogers and how I didn't really feel anything but this strange numbness when I did it. She assured me I'm definitely not a slut or anything, which I think I kind of knew anyway. She said the word *slut* is just another word boys use to control us; if we like sex, we're shamed for it, and it's completely natural to want sex and to enjoy it. She says what happened with Tom has left me pretty mixed up about what a real relationship is supposed to be like. And yes, in case you're wondering, I do still want a boyfriend. In fact, there's this really nice guy that everyone calls DJ who moved here from Backhurst. His parents go to our church. He's got red hair and freckles, and when he smiles at me I just about melt inside. He told me he was fully cut that I was moving, but he says we have to hang when I come home for the holidays. (I love the way he talks!) And he just got his P plates and says he'll even drive interstate to see me. Well, if his parents let him borrow their car. Can you believe it? We're not officially on together or anything yet, but I can't help thinking about what it would be like to kiss him. I try not to think too much further ahead than that, because then I get a bit scared.

Dr Cartwright says if I'm honest with DJ from the start and we take things slow, well ... She says if he really loves me he'll understand. And if he doesn't, he's just not the right guy for me. Dr Cartwright says she's confident it'll work out just fine because there are plenty of guys in the world who aren't anything like Tom. She says most guys just want to be loved—the same way we girls do. She says it might take a little while for me to start to truly believe that.

I still haven't told my parents about what happened with Tom. The police said there was no need to rush it or to force myself into something I wasn't ready for. I'd tell them when I was strong and ready. I was in control of who I told, when I told them, and how much I told them. I had several safe people to turn to—the people who knew about the rape. See—I can say the R-word now. I had a lot to work through, and the main thing was I was getting help. I had to congratulate myself on being strong.

I didn't want to be like Anne-Marie—unable to speak or set herself free. Anne-Marie probably felt she didn't have anyone to support her—nobody she felt she could talk to. The overwhelming shame robbed her of her will to live. She coped how she knew to, I guess. But to my mind there were also many good things to live for. Suicide just perpetuated the hurt and wrecked more people's lives—especially the lives of the people you love. I wasn't about to give up and have Tom steal my life away on top of everything else he stole from me.

What happened with Tom would always be part of me. It would affect the way I thought about the world and about people I met in the future. It would play a role in relationships, not only with boyfriends, but with family, friends, and the people I spent my working life with. I had to forgive myself and know that healing would take time. Maybe even a whole lifetime, but in the meantime I could congratulate myself on being a survivor. Maybe one day, when I was good and ready, I would consider legal action against Tom, but I was in the driver's seat now—and I could steer this any way I wanted. This was my choice—no one else's.

'Edwina, I said I love you, sweetheart.' Mum looked at me expectantly, as if she needed to hear me say it too.

I smiled at her. 'I love you too, Mum.' I said, taking her hand. She looked relieved and squeezed my hand.

I would tell her one day—in a way she could understand. I couldn't tell her now because I knew how she would react. She'd be angry and make a big song and dance about it. I'm not saying she didn't have a right to be angry at Tom. It's just that I was dealing with my own feelings right now and I wasn't strong enough to deal with hers as well. It would just be too much. Small, slow steps. That's what Dr Cartwright says. She told me I might not be able to control situations—but I can control the way I deal with things. It was important to recognise I couldn't control my mum and her reaction, but I could save it for a time when I knew I could deal with it.

As for Tom, well, I kind of saw him differently now. I didn't see him as a monster. I saw him as pathetic. A full-grown man who had preyed on a young girl for sex. What did that say about him? What sort of person was he? A man with no self-confidence to make it with girls of his age? A man who cared about his own self-gratification at the expense of anyone else? He was not a good human being—he was an opportunist who looked out for number one. He would have to know what he did was wrong. I hope the idea that he could one day pay for his actions haunts him. I hope it haunts him every day like he haunts me.

Dr Cartwright said what goes around comes around. And I had no doubt in my mind that Tom's time would come—I would make sure of that. It was only a matter of time.

ACKNOWLEDGMENTS

I would like to acknowledge Dyan Blacklock, former publisher at Omnibus Books, Scholastic. Dyan, you made the gutsy and defiant move to first publish this novel in 2007 and I am forever grateful.

Thank you to Matt Rubinstein for printing this new edition, and for recognising its value in light of the Australian government's recent decision to adopt changes to the curriculum to teach consent.

My ongoing thanks to my darling friend, Andrea Altamura. You read this manuscript some twenty years ago—my first ever—and you're still here by my side, living my publication journey with me. My eternal thanks to Vikki Wakefield for helping to make dreams on paper a reality. Thank you to my agent Jane Novak, and to my bookings agent, Becky Lucas. I have the best team imaginable. And finally, thank you to my husband and son: there *are* good men in the world and you're two of the very best.

Allayne L. Webster is an internationally published Children's and Young Adult author. She also plays guitar/sings and sometimes she illustrates.

Allayne is the proud recipient of three arts grants and a South Australian Premier's Reading Challenge Ambassador. She has served on literary festival boards and her novels have been listed for various awards.

Paper Planes (Scholastic) was a 2016 CBCA Notable, shortlisted for the Adelaide Festival Awards, and has recently been included in the Australian Heritage Literary Project *Untapped* Collection. *A Cardboard Palace* (MidnightSun Publishing) was a 2018 CBCA Notable, published in Sweden. *Our Little Secret* (Scholastic) was listed for the Golden Inkys, and *The Centre of My Everything* (Penguin Random-House) was listed in the 2019 Davitt Awards and shortlisted in the 2020 Adelaide Festival Awards. *Sensitive* (UQP) is published in Russia and was shortlisted in the 2020 Australian Speech Pathology Awards.

That Thing I Did – YA (Wakefield Press) was published in 2022 and *Selfie* – YA (Text Publishing) will be out 2023.

ALSO BY ALLAYNE L. WEBSTER

Junior Fiction

Barnesy
Sam's Surfboard Showdown
(co-authored with Amanda Clarke)

Middle Grade

A Cardboard Palace
Paper Planes

Young Adult

Stresshead
The Centre of My Everything
Sensitive
That Thing I Did
Selfie

For More Information

Website · www.allaynewebster.com
Facebook · allaynewebsterauthor
Twitter · allayne_webster
Instagram · allaynewebster

PRAISE FOR ALLAYNE L. WEBSTER

Praise for *That Thing I Did*

'Webster's wonderfully outrageous, crudely perceptive offering about growing up on the road surrounded by oddball friends should not be missed.'

—*Australian Book Review*

'Such a joyful ride filled with adventure and romance—5 stars!'

—*Good Reading Magazine*

'A wild ride from start to finish: it's witty, hilarious, hectic, manic and unabashedly irreverent!'

—Holden Sheppard, author of *Invisible Boys*

'It's a hot mess of the best possible kind, and well worth the ride. If you do one thing this year, read *That Thing I Did*. I loved this book.'

—Erin Gough, author of *Amelia Westlake*

'Bawdy bonkers brilliance, and a book you'll never forget, for all the wickedly right reasons.'

—Adam Cece, author of *Huggabie Falls*

'Along the way there are a lot of mishaps, corny jokes and laughs galore, but at the same time Webster completely handles more serious issues of suicide, abuse, and difficult relationships.'

—Helen Eddy, *ReadPlus*

Praise for *Sensitive*

'*Sensitive* combines laugh-out-loud moments with the seriousness of being thirteen. I loved it.'

—Emily Gale, author of *I am Out With Lanterns*

'Strong, funny, SJ will win your heart, even as her situation breaks it.'

—Bren McDibble, author of *How to Bee*

'Honest, funny-sad and real, *Sensitive* is an unforgettable story about living with chronic illness, and about being yourself when all you really want is to be somebody else.'

—Vikki Wakefield, author of *This is How We Change The Ending*

Praise for *The Centre of My Everything*

'Both heartbreaking and heart-warming. Allayne Webster navigates the world of young adults living in a regional town with a deft hand and sharp eye. The characters are raw and beautifully realised and stay with you long after reading. I was hooked from the first page.'

—Sue Lawson, author of *Freedom Ride*

'A gut-punch of honesty with a sting in the tail.'

—Dianne Touchell, author of *A Small Madness*

'*The Centre of My Everything* will draw you in and warm your soul.'

—Nicole Hayes, author of *One True Thing*

Praise for Allayne's other novels

'Lively, believable characters and positive role models for teenagers.'

—*The Advertiser*

'An incredible insight into the confused mind of someone who is little more than a child, and how adults can easily manipulate them but misunderstand and underestimate them.'

—*Brisbane Courier Mail*

'Shows you can grow and change, and winning isn't everything.'

—*Reading Time* Magazine

'Webster uses language that will resonate with teenagers, yet she writes with skill and beauty. Funny, clever, honest.'

—*Good Reads* Magazine

'Webster has woven a believable, credible tale that successfully draws its female readers into the character and captures the teenage voice.'

—*Magpies* Magazine

'Unflinching, important, beautifully written, highly recommended.'

—*Reading Time* Magazine

'Hard to put down, gripping, moving, deliberately confronting.'

—*The Advertiser*

COPYRIGHT

First published in 2007 by Omnibus Books

This edition published in 2022
by Ligature Pty Limited

34 Campbell St · Balmain NSW 2041 · Australia
www.ligatu.re · mail@ligatu.re

e-book ISBN 978-1-922749-66-6
print ISBN 978-1-925883-48-0

ligature finest

www.ingramcontent.com/pod-product-compliance
Ingram Content Group Australia Pty Ltd
76 Discovery Rd, Dandenong South VIC 3175, AU
AUHW020639050325
407891AU00002B/4

9 781925 883480